"Don't you think Tiny will make it?"

"But will they be cured?" Mr. Pollard asked anxiously. "My pigs aren't going to die, are they?"

"No, Luke. Antibiotics are wonderful things. I see no reason why they shouldn't all grow up to be fine, healthy specimens — or most of them, anyway."

Val saw him glance at the runt.

"Don't you think Tiny will make it?" she asked.

"If you mean small-fry here, it's anybody's guess how well he'll do. There's a runt in every litter. Sometimes they manage to compete with their bigger brothers and sisters, but often there just isn't enough milk to go around. But we'll give him a shot just like the others. He'll just have to take his chances."

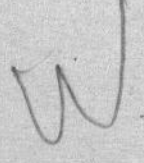

Look for these books in the Animal Inn series from Apple Paperbacks:

#1 *Pets Are for Keeps*
#2 *A Kid's Best Friend*
#3 *Monkey Business*
#4 *Scaredy Cat*
#5 *Adopt-A-Pet*
#6 *All the Way Home*

ANIMAL INN

ALL THE WAY HOME

Virginia Vail

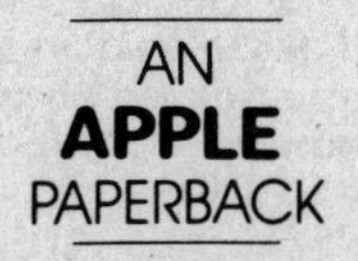

SCHOLASTIC INC.
New York Toronto London Auckland Sydney

ISBN 0-590-43430-6

Published by Scholastic Inc. APPLE PAPERBACKS
is a registered trademark of Scholastic Inc.

12 11 10 9 8 7 6 5 4 3 2 1 9/8 0 1 2 3/9

Printed in the U.S.A.

First Scholastic printing, August 1987

Chapter 1

"Okay, Mr. Radford, you can take Prince home now."

Val Taylor dug in her sneakered heels as the sturdy brindle boxer lunged happily toward his master. The dog was so strong that he almost pulled Val off her feet. The inflammation that had been making the boxer limp painfully was completely cured, and Prince was as frisky as a puppy.

Mr. Radford took the leash from Val, patted Prince's sleek head, and ordered him to sit.

"Thanks, Val. You tell your dad thanks, too. I was sure old Prince was going to be lame for life. You tell Doc Taylor he's the best vet in Pennsylvania — maybe in the whole United States!"

"I will, Mr. Radford," Val said, smiling. "I think so, too."

She opened the door of Animal Inn's waiting room, then closed it behind Mr. Radford and Prince as they went out. Mr. Radford's praise made her feel good. Val was very proud of her father. She only hoped that when she was a veterinarian, she'd be able to care for sick or injured animals as well as he did. But Val knew she still had a long, long way to go. Now she was learning everything she could by working at her father's side several days a week after school and on weekends.

"Hey, Val, let's clean up. I've got a lot of homework to do tonight."

Toby Curran, Doc's other young assistant and one of Val's best friends, came into the waiting room carrying a mop and pail. Prince was the last patient of the day, and it was time to wash the floor and the benches.

"Okay."

Val yawned and stretched, then reached for the mop. It had been a busy day at Animal Inn, and she was tired. But she knew that cleaning up was as much a part of her job as caring for her father's animal patients. Val didn't really enjoy clean-up duty, but she knew it had to be done.

"I'll mop, you sponge," she said.

Toby took the sponge she tossed at him and began scrubbing the benches and tables while Val started mopping the floor.

Rrrriiinngg!

It was the telephone at the reception desk. Val glanced at her watch. Quarter after five. Must be an emergency, she thought as she stuck the mop back into the pail and ran to get the phone. Animal Inn's office hours ended at five, so anyone who called after that must have something very important to say — something that needed Doc's immediate attention.

"Good afternoon — Animal Inn. May I help you?" she said. "Oh, hi Mr. Pollard. This is Val. . . . Yes, Doc's still here. What's wrong? . . . Oh, dear. I'm sorry to hear that. *All* of them?"

"What's up?" Toby asked.

Val covered the mouthpiece of the phone and said, "It's Sadie Pollard, Mr. Pollard's prize sow. Sadie's babies are. . . . Yes, Mr. Pollard, I'm right here. Yes, I'm writing it all down. Sadie had a litter of ten piglets six weeks ago, and now they're all wheezing and gasping and they won't eat. Sadie's fine, but the piglets are. . . . Yes, Mr. Pollard, I'll tell him right away."

She checked Doc's appointment book.

"No, he doesn't have any other calls to make tonight. We can come to your farm in about half an hour, okay? . . . Good. We'll see you then."

She hung up the phone.

"What's wrong with Sadie's piglets?" Toby asked.

"You heard me say they're wheezing and gasping, and they won't nurse, right?"

Toby nodded.

"Well, Mr. Pollard's afraid they might die. We have to get over to the Pollard pig farm right away. I have to tell Dad."

"You go ahead. I'll finish cleaning up," Toby said. "Mike will be here any minute, and he can help me."

Mike Strickler was Animal Inn's night man, an elderly jack-of-all-trades who always reminded Val of a leprechaun — even though he came from pure Pennsylvania Dutch stock.

Val went into the treatment room, where she found Doc Taylor washing up.

"Dad, I just got a call from Luke Pollard," Val said. "Sadie's new litter is sick. He wants you to come over there right away."

Doc sighed. "All right. Get my bag, Vallie, and meet me at the van."

A few minutes later, Val was seated next to Doc in the Animal Inn vet van, heading down the York Road.

"What do you think Sadie's piglets have?" Val asked.

"Can't tell until we see them," Doc said. "Luke Pollard's a good farmer. He never calls unless there's something he can't handle. Sounds like B.B. to me."

"What's B.B.?" Val asked.

"*Bordetella broniseptica,*" said Doc. "It's a respiratory disease that piglets get sometimes, particularly young piglets, like Sadie's litter. If it gets to their lungs, it can lead to pneumonia. I'm surprised that Luke's piglets have come down with it. None of his ever have before."

"Are they going to die?"

"Not necessarily — not if Mr. Pollard has contacted us in time. But it's very contagious. If there are other litters, they may be in danger, too."

Val bit her lip, hoping that Doc would be able to save Sadie's litter. Sadie was a nice pig, and Val knew she'd be upset if her piglets got pneumonia and died.

Mr. Pollard was waiting for them when they pulled into the barnyard. He looked worried.

"Right this way, Doc," he said. He glanced at Val and smiled. "I see you've brought your assistant. How you doing, Vallie?"

"Fine, thank you, Mr. Pollard. Just fine."

Val followed Doc and Mr. Pollard to Sadie's pen. The big sow was lying on clean, fresh straw, and ten roly-poly piglets were snuggled up next to her — or rather, nine roly-poly ones and one scrawny little runt. All of the piglets were breathing very hard. Sadie didn't look very happy, either.

"Don't know what's wrong with them, Doc," Mr. Pollard said. "I've never had a problem like this before."

Doc went into the pen and began to examine

the piglets. Val knelt beside him, stroking their fat little pink bodies. They kept on wheezing and coughing. Val felt very sorry for them, particularly for the runt. He was so small that it seemed impossible for him to survive any illness at all. Mr. Pollard looked on with concern.

"It's not pneumonia, is it?" he asked.

Doc shook his head. "Not yet. But it could turn into pneumonia. Good thing you called me when you did, Luke. Vallie, get me ten hypodermic needles and the antibiotics. We're going to give each one of these little fellows a shot of sulfa."

Val hurried to obey her father's orders as he added, "If I didn't know what good care you take of your pigs, Luke, I'd say they picked up this infection from dust in the air, or from damp, overcrowded conditions. As it is, they must have caught it from another animal. Any of your other pigs sick?"

"Nosirree!" Mr. Pollard said. "All healthy as can be. Like you said, Doc, I run a real clean pig farm. Why, I've seen people's houses that aren't as clean as my pig barn! Most folks think pigs are dirty animals, but they're not. Only reason they like to roll in the mud come summer is to cool off on a hot day. No, these are the only sick pigs I got."

As Val handed Doc another syringe, a small, fat black and white cat strolled into the pen. She reached out and patted it as it walked by.

"Who's this, Mr. Pollard?" she asked. "I've never seen this cat before."

"Oh, that's Midnight. She was a stray — just wandered into the barn one day and settled right in. Loves my pigs, Midnight does."

As though to prove him right, Midnight went over to the piglets and snuggled down between two of the plumpest ones.

"Don't know if it's really the pigs she's crazy about, or the warmth," Mr. Pollard went on. "I keep that heat lamp going most of the time so they don't catch a chill."

"Looks like she's got a cold, too," Val said. She'd noticed that the cat's eyes and nose were runny.

"She must've caught it from the pigs, I guess," said Mr. Pollard.

Doc looked up from the piglet he had just inoculated, a frown on his bearded face. "Val, hand me that cat, will you please?" he asked.

"Sure, Dad." Val picked up Midnight and gave the cat to her father. "Are you going to give her a shot, too?"

Doc peered into the cat's eyes, then took an instrument out of his bag and examined her ears. "Yes, I sure am," he said. "Luke, I think we've got the culprit right here."

"What do you mean?" asked Mr. Pollard. He looked puzzled.

"I mean that it's very doubtful that Midnight caught her cold from the piglets. It's much more likely that *they* were infected by *her*. I told Vallie on the way over here that your pigs' symptoms sounded very much like a respiratory disease called B.B. Now that I've become acquainted with Midnight here, I'm positive of it. Cats are well known to be carriers of the disease."

"Well, what do you know!" Mr. Pollard said. "Who'd have thought one little cat could make ten piglets sick? What should I do with her, Doc?"

"First, I'm going to give her a shot of sulfa. Then you're going to have to make sure she keeps far away from her friends from now on, or at least until all the animals are completely cured."

"But they *will* be cured?" Mr. Pollard asked anxiously. "My pigs aren't going to die just because a cat sneezed on them, are they?"

"No, Luke. Antibiotics are wonderful things. I'll be back in a few days to check them all out and give them another inoculation. I see no reason why they shouldn't all grow up to be fine, healthy specimens — or most of them, anyway."

Val saw him glance at the runt.

"Don't you think Tiny will make it?" she asked. She didn't know where the name came from. It had just popped into her head.

Doc picked up the little animal. "If you mean

small-fry here, it's anybody's guess how well he'll do. There's a runt in almost every litter. Sometimes they manage to compete with their bigger brothers and sisters and get enough to eat, but often there just isn't enough milk to go around, or if there is, the others are too greedy to let him have his share. But we'll give him a shot just like the others. He'll just have to take his chances."

"That's the way it is, all right," Mr. Pollard agreed. "Or sometimes the mother rolls over and smothers him." He saw Val's horrified expression and added, "Now don't get all upset, Vallie. It doesn't happen often, and old Sadie here would never harm one of her babies on purpose. But if one of them doesn't survive, it'll probably be the little guy — what did you call him?"

"Tiny," Val said softly around the lump in her throat.

"Vallie, more antibiotic, please," Doc said. Automatically Val handed him another vial, but she never took her eyes off Tiny.

"Even if he does grow up," Mr. Pollard said, "chances are he'll always be undersized. Not much meat on a runt. Why, this one's not much bigger than a sausage right now!" He laughed, but Val didn't. She'd been trying very hard not to think about the fact that all these adorable little creatures would one day end up as ham, bacon, pork chops, and sausage.

That was the reason she refused to eat meat. She couldn't forget that every hot dog, drumstick, and sirloin steak had once been part of a healthy, happy animal.

It seemed to Val that Tiny was looking at her pleadingly. All his brothers and sisters were snuggled up to Sadie, nursing, but there was no room for him.

Val reached out and selected the biggest, fattest piglet. She moved him away and put Tiny in his place.

"Give the little guy a chance, Fatso!" Val said, and Mr. Pollard laughed again, louder this time.

"I declare, Vallie, you're funny," he said. "Maybe I ought to hire you as a nursemaid for that little pig!"

Val watched sadly as Fatso trotted right over to Tiny and shoved him out of the way. Even though Fatso was wheezing and coughing like the rest, she could tell that he was a survivor. But poor little Tiny. . . .

"Mr. Pollard, couldn't you maybe bottle-feed Tiny until he's a little bigger and stronger?" she asked hopefully.

Mr. Pollard shook his head. "Don't have time, Vallie. I got lots of other pigs to take care of, and I'm shorthanded as it is. Like Doc said, he'll have to take his chances." He saw Val's sorrowful expression and added, "I'm not hardhearted. Besides, it's not good business to lose one of Sadie's piglets — she's a fine sow, and her litters are all prime pork." (Val winced.) "But if I lose one out of ten, and that one's a runt, well, I'm still ahead of the game. People around here know that Pollard's Pork Products are the best. And that means I can't waste time on a skinny little fella that's never going to amount to much."

"Vallie, we're finished here," Doc said. "You heard what Mr. Pollard said. Don't get all emotional on me now. If you're going to be a vet when you grow up, you have to learn to accept certain facts of life — animal life. We've done what we can to make sure that these piglets don't come down with pneumonia. We just can't control what happens to them after that."

Val nodded and gathered up the discarded syringes and empty vials. She knew Doc was right, but her heart ached for the little runt. Tiny's future looked very bleak. He wouldn't die of B.B., but it looked like he'd starve to death sooner or later. Or Sadie might even roll over on him. No matter what happened, Tiny was doomed. And he was so small and cuddly! If only Doc would let her take him home, she was sure she could save him.

Val looked up at her father.

Doc met her anguished gaze and said, "No, Vallie. No way. Come on, honey. Time to go home."

Doc told Mr. Pollard that he'd be back in three days to examine the piglets again and give them another inoculation, and reminded Mr. Pollard to keep Midnight far away from his pigs. Then he and Val headed for the van.

As they drove through the twilight on their way back to the big stone house on Old Mill Road, Val was silent. Finally she said, "Dad, he's really a nice little pig. . . ."

Doc kept his eyes on the road. "Yes, he is. And at home we have two nice dogs, a nice fat cat, four hamsters, rabbits, chickens, a duck, and a canary, not to mention The Gray Ghost at Animal Inn."

The mention of The Ghost made Val smile a little. She'd saved the beautiful dapple gray horse from being put to sleep, and now he was her very own. She was lucky, all right. Nobody else she knew had their very own horse. But she couldn't stop worrying about Tiny.

"No pigs, Vallie. Understand?"

Val sighed. "Yes, Dad. I understand."

Chapter 2

"I thought you two would *never* get home!"

Val's younger sister, Erin, met them at the door. She'd had ballet class that afternoon after school, and was still in her leotard and tights, her silky blonde hair twisted up in a ballerina knot. She gave Doc a big hug and a kiss, and thrust an envelope into his hand.

"It's a letter from Aunt Peggy!" she told him. Aunt Peggy was Val's mother's sister. She lived in New York City, which Erin thought was the most exciting, wonderful place in the whole world. The girls' mother had died in an automobile accident three years earlier, plunging the family into a grief from which they thought they would never recover. But it was a little better now, and Aunt Peggy had always kept in touch. A letter from Aunt Peggy was always filled with interesting news.

Now Erin leaped up and down, eager for her father to open the letter.

"Read it right now, Daddy," she urged. "I can't

wait to hear what she has to say!" She looked at Val. "What's the matter, Vallie? You look sad."

Val shrugged. "Nothing much. We went out to Mr. Pollard's pig farm — Sadie Pollard's piglets are sick. But they're going to be okay . . . except for Tiny."

"Who's Tiny?" Erin asked, but before Val could answer, Erin turned back to Doc. "Sit down in your favorite chair, Daddy, and read Aunt Peggy's letter."

Doc allowed himself to be led to the wing chair by the fireplace and began to open the envelope.

"Where's Teddy?" he asked. Teddy was Val and Erin's eight-year-old brother.

"Over at Eric's. Eric has a new video game. He'll be back any minute. *Read* it, Daddy!"

Val flopped down on the sofa, patting Jocko, the shaggy little black-and-white mongrel and Sunshine, the big golden retriever. Cleveland, her fat orange cat, leaped onto her lap and began purring happily.

"C'mon, Dad. What's new with Aunt Peggy?" she asked.

Doc skimmed the letter, and his shaggy eyebrows rose.

"Well, well!" he said at last.

"Daddy!" Erin wailed. "Will you just read it out loud?"

"Okay, here goes." Doc settled himself more comfortably, and began to read. " 'Dear Ted. Now that spring vacation's coming up, I've suddenly gotten an inspiration. I haven't seen you or your family for months, and the time has come for us to get together. I know how busy you always are, so I don't expect you to alter your schedule to fit in a trip to New York. But Valentine and Erin will be free for almost two weeks. Can I borrow them? I would absolutely *adore* to have them come and visit us here. We'll take them to the theater, the ballet — ' "

"Fantastic!" Erin cried.

" ' — the opera, the museums — all the wonderful events they must miss so sorely in Essex, Pennsylvania.

" 'You'll notice that I haven't included my nephew Teddy in this invitation. That's because I have a favor to ask in return. I'd love it if Milton, who's just Teddy's age, could spend the vacation with you and Teddy in Essex. It would be the best thing in the world for Milton, who, as a city kid and an only child, would benefit immensely from seeing how the rest of the world lives. Milton is much too serious, and a little shy. If Teddy is still as bouncy and outgoing as I remember him, he'd do Milton a world of good.

" 'Do phone me as soon as you can. I'm dying to see my nieces. We'll have lots of fun, as I'm sure Milton will with Teddy. Love to you and all the inhabitants of Animal Inn, Peggy.' "

"Oh, Daddy, can we go?" Erin cried. "Please say we can! We'll see the New York City Ballet and the Joffrey and maybe the American Ballet Theatre. . . ! Oh, Vallie, won't it be super?"

Val snuggled Cleveland closer to her chest. "I don't know, Erin. In New York City, all the animals are in zoos. And I *hate* zoos!"

"But you see animals all the time here at home," Erin said. "In New York, you'd see stuff that's so much more exciting! The policemen ride *horses* there, Vallie! Daddy, you'll let us go, won't you?"

"Well, I don't know," Doc said, rubbing his beard. "I'll have to give it some thought."

Just then the front door burst open and Teddy dashed in, his cheeks flushed and his golden-brown curls wild under the Phillies baseball cap he always wore.

"Hi, Dad! I wiped out a billion Martians on Eric's new video game! I'm the champion Star Blast player!"

The dogs galloped over to him and began jumping up and licking his face. Teddy rolled on the floor, giggling, and barking back at Jocko and Sunshine. When he got to his feet, he saw the letter in Doc's hand.

"Who's that from?" he asked.

"Aunt Peggy!" Erin said. "Val and I are going to New York for spring vacation!"

"Yeah? Neat!" Teddy picked up Jocko and swung

him around in circles. "I don't have to go, do I? I don't wanna go to New York."

"How'd you like to have your cousin Milton come to visit you?" Doc asked.

Teddy put Jocko down. "My cousin Milton? You mean that wimpy little kid with the glasses? Yuck!"

Doc gave him a look. "You haven't seen your cousin Milton in three years, Teddy. Aunt Peggy thought it would be a good idea if you and Milton get reacquainted."

"Sounds gross to me," Teddy said. "But it's better than going to New York. You want to go to New York, Vallie?"

Val sat up, clutching Cleveland. "Not very much," she admitted. She looked at her father. "I don't have to go if I don't want to, do I, Dad? Jill and I made all sorts of plans for vacation, and I want to work at Animal Inn full-time. Do I have to go?"

"Vallie, you are absolutely, positively *nuts*!" Erin cried. "Just think of what you'd be missing! The ballet, the theater, the opera! And the mounted policemen!"

Val buried her nose in Cleveland's soft, orange fur. "I'd rather stay here with Dad and ride The Ghost every day. You go if you want, Erin. You'll have a great time. I just want to stay here where I belong."

Erin's face fell. "Daddy, if Vallie doesn't want to go, does that mean I can't go, either?"

"Not necessarily." Doc stood up. "I have to think about this. But in the meantime, I'm starved. What's for dinner?"

Before Erin could reply, a blood-curdling shriek came from the kitchen.

"That's Mrs. Racer!" Val cried. "It sounds like something awful has happened!"

She led the way to the kitchen, where Mrs. Racer, the Taylors' elderly housekeeper, was standing in the middle of the room, pointing with a trembling finger at the kitchen table.

"What's the matter, Mrs. Racer?" Val asked anxiously. "Are you sick or something?"

"Cottage cheese! Cottage cheese!" Mrs. Racer wailed. "Spider! Cottage cheese!"

"Calm down, Mrs. Racer," Doc said, putting an arm around her quaking shoulders. "What's wrong?"

"Hey, you found Herman!" Teddy shouted, running over to the butcher block table and peering into the plastic cottage cheese container that sat there. "I was real worried about him! Thanks a lot!"

Val and Erin came over to peer over Teddy's shoulder. In the plastic container was a very large, very hairy tarantula.

"Yuck!" Erin cried.

"Hey, that's a neat tarantula," Val said. "Where'd you get him?"

Teddy stroked the tarantula with one finger. The

spider was a little groggy, and didn't respond.

"My teacher asked if somebody could take Herman home for the holiday," Teddy said. "So I told her I could, and I brought him home today in his house." He beamed at Mrs. Racer. "The cottage cheese container is his house. If you look close you can see the little airholes we made so he can breathe. He's a real neat spider. I brought him in here this afternoon after school, and I guess I left him on the table. Only Eric had this great video game, so I kind of forgot about him. Where'd you find him?"

Mrs. Racer had calmed down enough to speak, though her voice trembled a little. "In the refrigerator, that's where. I thought it was cottage cheese, but when I opened it. . . ." She shuddered. "If there's one thing I can't stand, it's spiders! Terrible, sneaky things, with all them legs! And *this* is the biggest, hairiest spider I ever saw in all my born days!"

Teddy leaned down and peered closely at Herman. "How'd he get into the refrigerator? He doesn't look too good. I hope he doesn't catch cold!"

"*I* put him in the refrigerator," Erin said. She shuddered, too. "If I'd known that — that *thing* was in there, I wouldn't have touched it with a ten-foot pole! I wondered why there were holes in the lid! That was a horrible, nasty trick, Teddy Taylor! Why, Mrs. Racer might have had a heart attack or something!"

Val joined Teddy and looked at the spider. "I'm not crazy about tarantulas, but he's a nice, big, fat one," she said. "But he can't stay in that little plastic cup. Hey, I know! My old aquarium is down in the basement someplace. We could bring it up — "

"Stop right there!" Doc commanded. "We are *not* keeping this tarantula. You know the rules, Teddy. No new pets unless everyone agrees. Not even temporary ones. Herman goes back tomorrow morning — no ifs, ands, or buts. Why did you bring him home so soon, anyway, Teddy? Spring vacation doesn't start for another two weeks."

"Well. . . ." Teddy tugged at the visor of his baseball cap. "Mrs. Robinson doesn't 'zactly like Herman. She says he gives her the creeps. One of the kids in my class brought him in for Show and Tell a couple of weeks ago, and then he never came back. He moved, or something."

"Smart kid," Doc said dryly. "Sorry, Teddy. I sympathize with Mrs. Robinson, but she'll have to find another home for Herman. Put the lid back on and take him up to your room. And tomorrow, you will return him." He looked down at Mrs. Racer. "Are you all right, Mrs. Racer?" he asked.

She nodded her white head. "So long as I know that critter won't be here when I come tomorrow morning, I'll be fine." She adjusted the little white lawn cap she always wore and smoothed her apron.

"I don't mind cats and dogs, or rabbits and chickens, either. And that little monkey was cute as she could be. But spiders — I can't work in a house with big, hairy spiders, no sir!"

Teddy sighed and put the lid back on Herman's house.

"C'mon, Herman," he said. "We're going up to my room. You can talk to my hamsters." He trudged out of the kitchen, his shoulders slumped. "Don't feel bad," Val heard him say as he went through the dining room. "*I* like you, even if nobody else does."

"He *is* kind of a nice spider," she said.

"No spiders, Vallie, and *no pigs*," Doc said firmly.

"Pigs?" Erin echoed. "What do you mean, no pigs?"

"Never mind," Val said sadly. If she'd had even the faintest glimmer of hope that Doc might change his mind and let her adopt Tiny, it was gone now. "What's for supper, Mrs. Racer?"

"Pork chops," Mrs. Racer replied promptly. "And a vegetable casserole for you, Vallie." She took off her apron and hung it on the hook on the kitchen door. "I'll just get my coat. M'son Henry'll be here any minute."

Pork chops! Val thought. A picture formed in her mind of all those little pink pigs. She remembered the sign on the side of Mr. Pollard's delivery truck, the one he used to take his meat to the markets in town. POLLARD'S PORK PRODUCTS, it said. Underneath the writing was a picture of a smiling pig doing a jig on its hind legs. Val suddenly didn't feel very hungry, even for vegetable casserole.

"Daddy, can I go?" Erin asked later that night. The Taylors were finishing their supper, and Val was serving big, juicy wedges of Mrs. Racer's coconut cream pie.

"Go where?" Doc replied absentmindedly.

"To New York! To stay with Aunt Peggy. Just because Vallie doesn't want to go, that doesn't mean I can't, does it? I'm old enough to take the train by myself — I'm eleven going on twelve. That's old enough."

"I said I'd think it over," Doc said. "And I haven't had much time to think, thanks to Herman."

Teddy gave him a look, then dug into his pie. "I think you oughta let her go, Dad," he said through a mouthful of coconut cream. "And you probably oughta let Milton come here. Maybe he wouldn't be so wimpy if he hung around with the guys for a while."

"You sure you don't want to go with Erin?" Doc asked Val.

"I'm sure. I don't like New York. And Jill and I have lots of things we want to do, and you said I could work full-time." She smiled at Erin. "But Erin really ought to go. She'd love it. I bet Aunt Peggy would take her to the ballet every single night!"

"Oh, Daddy, please?" Erin begged. "If I'm going to be a ballerina like Mommy was, I have to see the best dancers in the world, and they all perform in New York City. If I don't go, I'll *never* be a ballerina, I just know it."

Doc polished off the last of his pie. "I don't see why not," he said at last. Erin and Val exchanged happy glances across the table. "And I think it's a good idea for Milton to come here. I'll write to Aunt Peggy tonight."

"Phone!" Erin cried eagerly. "Call her right now! Right this very minute!" She grabbed the receiver of the wall phone next to the kitchen table and thrust it at her father.

"I'll get the number," Val said, running into the dining room. She picked up Doc's address book and handed it to Doc. He turned to Aunt Peggy's number.

"Might as well," he said. "I obviously won't have any peace until I do."

Erin danced around impatiently while he dialed. Val began to clear the table and Teddy helped her put the plates in the dishwasher.

Finally, "Peggy? It's Ted. Just got your letter, and it looks as though you have yourself a guest. . . . Yes, that's right — one. Vallie wants to stay here, but Erin's ready to leave right now."

"I can't wait," Erin shouted into the receiver. "Thanks so much for inviting us!"

Doc and Aunt Peggy spoke some more, making travel arrangements. Then Doc said, "And we're looking forward to having Milton come to stay with us. It'll be good for our boys to get to know each other again — "

"Ask her if Milton's still a wimp," Teddy said loudly, and Val winced.

Doc scowled at him, shaking his head vigorously. "Yes, that was Teddy," he said. "What did he say? Uh . . . he said that Milton is quite an imp."

Val, Erin, and Teddy snorted with suppressed laughter while Doc looked daggers at them all.

After further conversation about train schedules, dates, and times, Doc hung up.

"Milton's an *imp*. Right, Dad!" Teddy giggled.

"You sure think fast, Dad," Val added, trying to keep a straight face.

But Doc was not amused. "That was very rude, Teddy," he said. "You haven't laid eyes on your cousin Milton in years. Granted, he wasn't as sturdy a child as you, but that's no reason to refer to him as a wimp. He might surprise you. It's entirely possible that he's grown into a big, tough kid who'll beat you to a pulp if you call him names. People change, you know."

"Okay, Dad. I'm sorry," Teddy said, looking

down at his sneakered feet. Then he brightened. "Hey, I wonder if Milton's a baseball fan! If he is, I bet he likes the Yankees, or maybe the Mets. 'Course, they're not as good as the Phils, that's for sure. I wonder if he collects baseball cards. Maybe we could trade."

"I think you ought to write him a letter," Doc suggested. "If Milton writes back, you'll get to know something about him before he arrives."

"That's a cool idea!" Teddy said. "Wonder if he has any pets? I bet he doesn't have a tarantula!"

"Neither do you," Doc reminded him. "Why don't you go upstairs right now and start that letter?"

"I will," said Teddy. "C'mon, guys," he called to Jocko and Sunshine. "We're going up to my room. I'll walk you when I finish my letter."

After Teddy and the dogs had galloped off, Erin flung her arms around Doc's neck and gave him a big kiss.

"Oh, Daddy, thanks for letting me go! This is the most exciting thing that's happened to me in my whole entire life!"

Doc held her close, then looked down at her, his expression serious.

"Are you really that eager to leave home, honey?" he asked.

The tone of his voice gave Val a funny feeling in the pit of her stomach. Why did he sound so sad? It wasn't like Erin was going away for good, only for ten days. It suddenly struck her that the family had never been separated before. Neither she nor Erin nor Teddy had ever even gone to sleep-away camp.

I'll miss her, Val realized. I'll miss her a whole lot.

"It's only for a little while, Daddy," Erin said. "And I'll send postcards every single day. Oh, it's going to be so wonderful!"

"Come on, Erin," Val said. "Time to feed the rabbits and the duck and Teddy's chickens."

Erin made a face. "Why can't Teddy feed his own chickens?"

"Because he's writing a letter to Milton. He'll feed them tomorrow night."

"Oh, all right," Erin said. "But when we're done, I'm going to call Olivia. She's going to be *green* with envy!"

"Then let *her* feed the chickens tomorrow night," Doc joked.

Erin gave her father a loving poke as she followed Val out the back door. "That's not what I mean, and you know it. You're such a tease!"

Val's funny feeling began to go away. It was just a little vacation, after all. Nothing was really going to change. . . .

Chapter 3

The next two weeks sped by so quickly that Val hardly knew they were gone. Whenever she could, she biked out to Mr. Pollard's pig farm to check on Tiny. He didn't seem to be getting any bigger, though the wheezing and coughing went away. The other piglets got fatter and fatter. Tiny seemed to be holding his own, but he didn't put on any weight. Val worried about him constantly. Toby said she was nuts.

"He's gonna be okay," he told her. "So what if he doesn't gain weight? He's alive, isn't he?"

Val had to admit he was, but she was sure that Tiny was always hungry. And if he didn't get enough to eat, he'd fade away and die, she just knew it.

At home, Erin was in a tizzy, preparing for her trip to New York. She'd decided that she didn't have the right clothes for her vacation, so Olivia's mother had taken her shopping. Erin came back with a wardrobe that was perfect for all the cultural events she was going to attend. Erin's favorite was a bright flowered dress with a full skirt and a white lace collar. It would look beautiful with white tights and her black patent leather flats with the bows.

"You ought to buy some dresses, Vallie," Erin said after her shopping trip. "All you ever wear is jeans and sweat shirts. And you ought to do something with your hair. You have such great hair — it's long and thick, and such a pretty color, not dishwater blonde like mine."

"Your hair's not dishwater blonde," Val said. "It's ash blonde, like Mom's was. And besides, when would I ever wear dresses? I'd look pretty silly in a skirt when I'm taking care of the patients at Animal Inn. And I couldn't ride The Ghost in a dress."

Erin sighed. "I wish you were coming with me, Vallie. I bet you'd like New York once you got used to it."

"But by the time I got used to it, we'd be on our way back home," Val pointed out. "No, I'll stay here with Dad. You'll have a wonderful time, Erin. And you can tell me all about it when you get home."

"When I'm a famous ballerina, I'll invite you to visit me in New York," Erin said. "But if you show up in those ratty old jeans. . . ."

"You won't let me in?" Val asked.

"Oh, I'll let you in, all right. But I'll have to tell my famous friends that you're my eccentric sister from Pennsylvania. I bet you'll be a big hit — like Miss Maggie is, here in Essex!"

Val thought about Miss Maggie Rafferty, the elderly lady who took in all the stray animals that the Animal Shelter didn't have room for. Miss Maggie was eccentric, all right, but she had a heart of gold. It wouldn't be so bad, being like her. Not bad at all.

All of a sudden, the day arrived when Erin was to leave for New York. Doc took her suitcase out to the car while Erin said good-bye to Mrs. Racer.

"You take real good care of yourself, Erin, hear?" Mrs. Racer said, hugging her tightly. "And don't you dare go anywhere by yourself. There's thieves and muggers and I don't know what all in New York City." She stroked Erin's sleek, light hair. "Oh, dear, I wish Vallie was going with you! What if your Aunt Peggy forgets to meet you at the train station?"

"She won't, Mrs. Racer," Erin assured her and kissed the old woman's wrinkled cheek. "I'm going to be just fine, honest."

"If she *does* forget, you just march yourself right over to the first policeman you see," Mrs. Racer went on as though Erin hadn't spoken. "And you give him your aunt's telephone number and he can call her up and tell her where you are. Did you write her number down?"

"Yes, Mrs. Racer," Erin said patiently. "It's right here in my purse."

"C'mon, Erin, let's *go!*" said Teddy, tugging at her sleeve.

"Don't worry, Mrs. Racer," Val said. "Erin'll be all right. And she's going to call us just as soon as she gets to Aunt Peggy's. Now we really do have to go, or else Erin will miss her train."

"Hmph!" Mrs. Racer snorted. "Wouldn't be the worst thing in the world if she did."

She gave Erin one last hug, then turned abruptly and marched into the house, dabbing at her eyes with the corner of her apron.

Teddy dashed ahead to the car, followed by Erin and Val. As Val looked at her little sister's slim, straight figure, she realized that Erin wasn't so little anymore. She was almost as tall as Mrs. Racer. That wasn't really very tall — not nearly as tall as Val. But Erin carried herself with the natural grace of a born dancer. It was obvious she was excited about her trip — she didn't even look back once.

Val climbed into the backseat next to Teddy as Erin got in the front, and Doc backed the car out of the driveway.

"I can't believe it!" Erin cried happily. "I'm really on my way! I'm really going to New York!"

"And Milton's coming to Essex," Teddy said. Milton's train was scheduled to arrive in Harrisburg half an hour after Erin's left. "He never answered my letter. I wonder what he'll be like?"

"He's probably wondering the same thing about you," Doc said. "But you'll both find out soon enough."

"Yep, we sure will. Boy — no school for ten whole days! We're gonna have a super time," Teddy cried excitedly. "We're gonna play baseball and maybe go fishing, and you said I could have Eric and Billy and Sparky sleep over one night, Dad. It's gonna be great!"

Erin turned around. "Aren't you going to miss me, Teddy?" she asked.

"No way!" Teddy said. "And you won't miss me, either, I bet. You're gonna be doing all those dopey girl-things with Aunt Peggy. I bet you won't miss any of us one bit."

Val wished that Erin would say she'd miss them all a whole lot, but she didn't.

Half an hour later they were all standing on the platform at the Harrisburg train station.

"When the conductor comes through, be sure to hand him your ticket," Doc said. "And ask him to tell you right before you come into Penn Station so you'll have time to gather your belongings."

"Oh, Daddy, I only have one little suitcase," Erin said. "You and Mrs. Racer act like I'm a baby or something! I'm eleven years old. Milton's coming all by himself, and he's only eight. If he can figure out where to get off, so can I."

She peered down the track, her face flushed with excitement.

"I think I hear the train!" she cried. "Listen! It's right on time!"

Val heard it, too — a kind of humming noise. The other passengers began picking up their bags, and Doc picked up Erin's suitcase. They all stepped back as the train pulled into the station and slowed to a halt.

"Here, Erin," Val said, thrusting the magazine she'd been carrying into her sister's hand. "It's the latest copy of *Ballet World*. I thought maybe you'd like to read it on the train."

"Oh, Vallie, thanks!" Erin cried. She flung her arms around Val's neck, and the two girls clung together for a moment. I wish she weren't going, Val thought. I'm going to miss my little sister!

"You'll take care of Dandy, won't you?" Erin asked. "Don't let Cleveland into my room, promise?"

"I promise," Val said. She knew how much Erin loved her canary.

Erin broke away from Val and gave Doc a big hug and a kiss. "I'll write you every day, honest I will. And I'll call the minute I get to Aunt Peggy's."

Teddy hung back, scuffing the toe of one sneaker on the platform. "G'bye, Erin," he mumbled. "I guess maybe I'll miss you — a *little* bit." He stuck out a grubby fist. "Here's some Life Savers. All different flavors. Just in case you get hungry."

"Tropical Fruit!" Erin cried. "My favorite!"

She took the candy, then paused. "Is it okay if I kiss you good-bye?"

"Only if you do it real quick," Teddy said.

Erin leaned down and kissed his chubby cheek. Suddenly Teddy threw his arms around her and squeezed her with all his might.

"Bye, Erin."

"Bye, Teddy."

Then Doc took Erin's hand and helped her up the steps of the railroad car. A moment later, he was back on the platform.

"She has a window seat," he said. "There she is — *wave*!"

Val and Teddy waved like mad, and Erin waved back. Val thought her face looked very small and pale behind the window of the train.

But happy. Very happy.

The last of the passengers boarded, and the train began to pull away. Doc hugged Val and Teddy next to him as they watched it disappear into the distance.

"Well, now," Doc said, when they could no longer see even the end of the train, "What say we go have some breakfast? I don't know about you guys, but I'm starved."

Val wasn't a bit hungry, but she nodded.

"I want pancakes and sausages and orange juice and hot chocolate," Teddy said.

As they started up the steps to the main level of the station, Val slipped her hand into Doc's.

"She's going to be all right, isn't she, Dad?" she asked.

Doc smiled down at her. "Yes, Vallie, she's going to be all right."

Half an hour later, they were standing on the opposite side of the platform, waiting for the express train from New York. As the train slid into the station, Teddy jumped up and down.

"Is that him?" he asked, as a little boy of about his own age stepped down onto the platform. But the little boy was quickly followed by an elderly couple.

Several other people got off, suitcases in hand, and were met by friends or relatives. Finally, just as the train was about to pull out, a small boy wearing horn-rimmed glasses and a navy blue blazer with a crest over the breast pocket emerged. He looked around anxiously, clutching a small duffel bag in both hands. The boy had neatly combed brown hair and he looked very anxious.

"I bet that's Milton," Val said.

"I bet you're right," Doc responded.

"Gimme a break!" Teddy groaned. "That kid looks like Super-Wimp."

"Appearances can be deceiving," Doc said, heading for the little boy. "Hi. You wouldn't happen to be Milton Williamson, would you?"

"Are you my Uncle Ted?" the boy asked.

"If you're Milton, I'm your Uncle Ted," Doc said. "And this is your cousin Teddy, and your cousin Valentine."

The boy thrust out a hand, which Teddy took.

"Hey, Milton, how ya doing?" he asked.

"Hello, Teddy," Milton said. "I'm very pleased to make your acquaintance."

"Likewise," Teddy mumbled. He turned to Val. "Vallie, this is Milton. *Cousin* Milton. Milton, the wimp," he whispered.

"Shut up, Teddy," Val hissed. She turned her very best smile on Milton.

"Hello, Milton. We're so glad you could come to stay with us for spring vacation."

"Thank you for asking me," Milton said. "I'm looking forward to spending the next several days with the Taylor family. My luggage is over there." He pointed to a small suitcase on the platform. "I would appreciate it if whoever carries that suitcase would be very careful. It contains my favorite video game, and the slightest bump could disorganize the circuits."

Doc slung the duffel bag over his shoulder.

"No problem, Milton," he said heartily. "Everything's going to be just fine. Follow me. Our car's parked not too far from here. Teddy, take Milton's suitcase."

"If it's all the same to you," Milton said, "I'd rather carry it myself. It also contains my electronic chess set."

Val could tell Milton didn't think Teddy was careful enough to be trusted with his suitcase.

"Electronic chess set?" Teddy echoed. "You mean, like, computerized?"

"Precisely," Milton said. "I never go anywhere without my computer chess board. My mother tells me that you're a chess player, Uncle Ted."

"Well, I used to be," Doc said. "I haven't played in a while, though. I'm probably pretty rusty. Maybe you can help me brush up on my game."

"I'd like that," Milton said as he struggled up the long flight of stairs that led to the waiting room, lugging the suitcase.

"You want me to help you with that?" Val asked.

But Milton shook his head. "No, thanks. I can manage."

When they reached the car, Val got in the front seat and Teddy and Milton got in the back, the suitcase between them. Doc pulled out of the parking lot and eased into traffic, heading for home.

"Did you have a good trip, Milton?" Val asked.

"Yes, it was very nice, thank you," Milton replied. "My father gave me a new book to read on the train, and I finished it just before we got to Harrisburg."

"You read a *whole book* all at once?" Teddy asked, amazed.

"Yes," said Milton. "Often. I like to read."

"Me, too," Val said. "What's your favorite book? Mine's *National Velvet* — or maybe *Black Beauty*. I love stories about animals."

"So do I. But I like stories about people, too. The one I just finished is called *Flash Fry, Private Eye*. It was funny."

Teddy scrunched down in his seat. "*I* like comic books," he said.

"My parents don't let me read comic books," Milton said.

"No kidding!" Teddy thought about that for a moment. "They must be awful strict."

"Not really. They just make a lot of rules for me because I'm an only child," Milton said matter-of-factly. "They keep telling me I'm all they've got and they want me to have the best of everything."

"Do you like being an only child?" Val asked.

"Oh, yes. I'm used to it, just the way you and Teddy and Erin are used to having each other."

"Don't you get lonely sometimes?" Teddy asked.

"No. I like to do things by myself. And I can play with my friends whenever I want to. I have a lot of friends in my school. Some of them even live in the same apartment building."

Teddy leaned on the suitcase, peering at his cousin from under the visor of his Phillies cap. "What do your friends call you?" he asked.

"They call me Milton," said Milton.

"Don't you have a nickname? Don't they call you something for short — like, my name's Theodore but everybody calls me Teddy, and *nobody* calls Vallie Valentine. How about Milt? Anybody call you Milt?"

Milton shook his head. "My name's Milton, and that's what everybody calls me." He paused. "Well, when I first got my glasses, some of the kids called me 'Four-eyes,' but they weren't my *real* friends."

"Four-eyes, huh?" Teddy mused aloud.

Val knew exactly what he was thinking. She turned around and glared at him. "Teddy. . . ."

"What about pets, Milton," Doc said loudly. "Do you have any pets?"

"Guppies."

Teddy groaned faintly. "Oh, brother!"

"We have lots of pets," Val said. "A cat, two dogs, a canary, four hamsters. . . ."

She chattered nonstop about the Taylors' menagerie for the rest of the drive, but neither Teddy nor Milton said another word.

Chapter 4

"Dad, this isn't going to work out," Val said that night. The boys had gone to bed early. Val and Doc had tucked them in, Teddy in his own bed and Milton in Erin's.

"We're very glad to have you with us, Milton," Doc had said. "I certainly enjoyed our chess game. Thanks for teaching me to play on your computer set."

"You're welcome, Uncle Ted," Milton said. He looked very small and kind of defenseless without his glasses, Val thought as she stood by the bed looking down at him.

"Tomorrow, you and Teddy are coming with Dad and me to Animal Inn," Val told him. "And then some of Teddy's pals are coming to the house after lunch. You'll like them. They're really nice kids."

She wondered if she should kiss him good-night, and decided against it. He didn't look as though he wanted to be kissed.

Doc smoothed Milton's hair back from his forehead.

"Well, good-night, Milton. See you in the morning."

"Good-night, Uncle Ted. Good-night, Vallie." Milton closed his eyes.

Doc turned off the light, and he and Val left the room. Val was about to close the door when she heard Milton say, "Would you mind leaving the door open, please? It's very dark in here."

"No problem," Val said. Then she and Doc went to Teddy's room.

Teddy was curled up in his bed, scowling. Val paused in the doorway. Something was different. What was it? The hamsters were scampering around in their Habitrail the way they always did. Teddy's clothes and toys were scattered all over the room, the way they always were. But something was missing. Suddenly she knew what it was. Teddy always slept with Fuzzy-Wuzzy, the old, moth-eaten teddy bear that had been passed from her, to Erin, and then to Teddy. And Fuzzy-Wuzzy was nowhere in sight.

"Where's Fuzzy-Wuzzy?" she asked.

Instead of answering, Teddy said, "Is Milton in bed?"

"Yes, he is," Doc said.

"Okay, then." Teddy reached way down under the covers and brought out the bear. "I didn't want the wimp to know about Fuzzy-Wuzzy," he explained. "I don't want him to think I'm as wimpy as *he* is!"

Doc sat down on the edge of the bed. "Teddy, I want one thing understood. You are *not* to refer to Milton as 'the wimp' — not to me, not to Vallie, and not to your friends. And most especially not to Milton."

"But, Dad, he *is* a wimp! He's the wimpiest wimp I ever saw!" Teddy wailed. "He's afraid of Cleveland and the dogs, and he doesn't know anything about baseball or football or *anything*. All he wants to do is read his dumb old books, play that dumb computer chess game, or practice the dumb piano!"

"Milton plays very well for a boy of his age," Doc said calmly. "That little piece he played before supper was written by Mozart when he was nine years old."

"Big deal!" Teddy mumbled. "I s'pose next you're gonna tell me Milton's some kind of genius or something. Well, I don't care if he is. I wish he'd go back to New York where he belongs. He's the most *boring* kid I ever met!"

"Teddy, you don't know him very well yet," Val put in. "I think he's very nice. Quiet, maybe, but nice."

"Oh, he's nice, all right. He's gonna nice me

to death!" Teddy said. "And we're stuck with him for ten whole days!"

"One of them is already over," Doc reminded him. "Nine to go."

"Boy, this is gonna be the worst spring vacation ever," Teddy sighed, snuggling up to Fuzzy-Wuzzy. "Can't we send him back home?"

"No, we cannot," Doc said firmly. "Milton is your cousin and my nephew. He's part of our family. Give him time, Teddy. Let him get used to us. He'll loosen up after a while."

"And that's another thing!" Teddy cried, sitting up. "Milton's the *neatest* kid I ever saw! His hair looks like it's glued to his head. It never gets messed up. And his jeans have creases down the front, and his sneakers are *pure white*!"

Doc glanced around Teddy's room. "A little neatness isn't such a terrible thing."

Teddy flopped back down. "Milton's not a little neat, he's a *lot* neat. He's like a little old man trying to pretend he's a kid!"

Val had a hard time keeping a straight face. Teddy was right on target — that was exactly the impression Milton gave. Trying not to smile, she came over to the bed. "Good-night, sleep tight . . ." she said.

". . . and don't let the bedbugs bite," Teddy finished. As she bent down to kiss him, he pulled back. "You didn't kiss the w — Milton, did you?"

"Nope," Val said.

"Okay."

He allowed her to kiss his cheek. Then he flung his arms around Doc.

"I'll try to get used to him, Dad," he said. "And I won't call him a wimp unless I forget."

Doc ruffled Teddy's brown curls. "Don't forget," he said sternly.

"I'll try not to," Teddy said, clutching Fuzzy-Wuzzy and lying down so Doc could tuck him in. "But a person can't remember *everything*. And if a person forgets something, it's not really his fault."

"Good-night, Teddy."

"G'night, Dad."

Val had followed Doc out of Teddy's room and down the hall to Doc's study. Now she sat on the floor at his feet, rubbing Cleveland's stomach.

"It's really not going to work out," she said again. "Teddy and Milton are like . . . like oil and vinegar. They'll never mix."

Doc smiled. "I think you mean oil and *water*, Vallie. But you know, if you put oil and vinegar together and shake them up, you get salad dressing. That's what we have to do — keep putting Teddy and Milton together. Sooner or later, they'll find they have something in common."

"I don't know," Val said. "Right now, the only

thing I can see that they have in common is that they're both boys."

"That's more than Teddy and Sparky had in common, and look at them now," Doc said. Sparky was a girl and a new friend of Teddy's. It had taken quite a while — and quite a few fights — before they had seen eye to eye. She sighed. "At least Erin sounded happy when she called this afternoon."

"Erin's going to be just fine. This is a wonderful opportunity for her."

"I guess so," Val mumbled.

"What's the matter, Vallie?" Doc asked. "Are you sorry you decided not to go?"

"Oh, no, Dad! That's not it. . . . It's just . . . well, I wish Erin missed us a little. It's like she doesn't care about us at all. And I miss *her* already. I think I started missing her even before she left."

"You know something, Vallie? I miss her, too," Doc confessed. "But I certainly don't want her to be sad and homesick, and I'm sure you don't, either. Of course she cares about us, but this is a very exciting, grown-up thing she's doing. I don't know about you, honey, but I'm very proud that Erin's mature enough to enjoy her trip so much."

"I guess," Val sighed. "But I'm sure not proud of Teddy! What're we going to do about those two boys, Dad?"

Doc rubbed his beard thoughtfully. "Well, I've

been thinking. Milton's only been here for less than a day, and we've been treating him like a special guest — which he is, of course. But maybe that's why he doesn't seem to be comfortable with us. From now on, let's try treating him like a member of the family, which he *also* is. He'll never feel at home if we don't relax and let him know that he doesn't have to be a little gentleman every single minute. Somewhere inside that button-down shirt and those knife-creased pants there's a real, live little boy. It's up to us to convince that little boy to burst out — have fun, get dirty."

"Get *dirty*? *Milton?*" Val echoed. She shook her head. "I don't know, Dad. He's so clean he squeaks."

Doc smiled and stroked her hair. "We'll see what we can do about that, Vallie. Tomorrow morning, let's start all over. Pretend he's Erin."

"You mean like give him chores to do and stuff like that?" Val asked.

"Exactly. Aunt Peggy wants him to see how the rest of the world lives. Well, we're going to show him."

Val was up bright and early the next morning. On weekends, breakfast was often Val's responsibility. When Teddy and Milton came downstairs, she was busily scrambling eggs.

"Hi, guys. Have a good night's sleep?" she asked cheerfully.

"I slept very well, thank you," Milton said.

"What's for breakfast?" Teddy asked. "I'm starvin' like Marvin!"

"Scrambled eggs and bacon," Val told him. "But before you eat, you and Milton have to take the dogs out for a walk."

Milton's eyes widened behind the horn-rimmed glasses. "Both of us?" he asked.

"Yep, both of you. Ever walked a dog before?"

"N-no," Milton said. "I don't know much about dogs."

"You don't have to know anything about dogs to take them for a walk," Teddy said. "All you do is snap the leash onto their collars and take 'em out the door." He fastened Jocko's and Sunshine's leashes and handed Jocko's to Milton. "C 'mon, Milton. Follow me!"

Jocko bounded after Teddy and Sunshine, pulling Milton behind him.

"He's very strong," Milton said faintly as Jocko dragged him out the door.

"Just don't let go of the leash," Teddy called over his shoulder. "Jocko loves to run. If you let him go, he'll end up in the next county!"

Val heard the front door slam behind them. So

far, so good. She carefully placed strips of bacon on a tray and put it in the microwave. Then she plopped a chunk of butter in the frying pan on the stove. By the time the boys got back, she thought, breakfast ought to be ready.

"'Morning, Vallie," Doc said, coming into the kitchen. "Where are Teddy and Milton?"

"Walking the dogs," Val said. "I think Milton's a little worried about walking Jocko, but he's doing it."

"Good!" Doc sat down at the butcher block table. "Something smells delicious."

"Bacon," Val said. "It's in the microwave. And I'm making scrambled eggs."

"Sounds delicious. How about some orange juice?"

"Coming right up!"

Val poured him a glass, then began scrambling the eggs. Maybe she wasn't the best cook in the world, but there was no way she could ruin scrambled eggs.

Twenty minutes later, the scrambled eggs were cooling in the frying pan, and the bacon had turned into hard little crisps.

"They should have been home long before this, unless they walked the dogs all the way across town," Doc said, looking at his watch.

"Maybe you'd better eat, Dad," Val said. "I'll wait and eat with the boys."

She slid a lump of scrambled eggs onto Doc's plate and carefully arranged several small hard bacon strips next to the yellow mound. At least the toast was fresh and hot. . . .

As Doc began gingerly eating his breakfast, the front door was flung open, and Sunshine galloped, tongue lolling, into the kitchen. A moment later, Teddy and Milton appeared, with Jocko still on his leash.

"Milton lost him!" Teddy yelled. "He dropped the leash, and Jocko's been running for miles and miles and *miles*! I thought we'd never catch him!"

"I'm very sorry," Milton said. "Jocko's a lot stronger than he looks. I've never walked a dog before."

"I *told* you, all you had to do was hang on," Teddy muttered. He looked at the plate Val put in front of him. "What's that?"

"Breakfast," Val said.

"What're those little hard things?"

"Bacon. It got a little crisp."

"Oh, boy," Teddy sighed.

Milton sat down at his place. "I'm not very hungry, Vallie."

"How about a piece of toast and some orange juice?" Val asked wearily.

"That would be very nice, thank you."

Val took two slices from the toaster and put them on a plate which she set in front of Milton.

"There's grape jelly," she said.

"You don't happen to have orange marmalade?" Milton asked hopefully.

"Yuck! Orange marmalade tastes like garbage!" Teddy muttered. "Jocko could've been hit by a *car*!"

"But he wasn't," Doc said. "Teddy, eat your eggs. Milton, here's the grape jelly. You'll love it."

"I'm sure I will, Uncle Ted," Milton said. He began spreading the jelly on his toast. "We usually have orange marmalade at home. My mother gets the kind that's imported from England."

"Mrs. Racer made the grape jelly," Teddy said through a mouthful of cold scrambled eggs. "She makes the best grape jelly in the world."

"I'm sure it's very nice," said Milton.

There was a long silence, during which all of them tried to pretend that they were enjoying their breakfast.

"Well!" Doc said at last. "Wonderful meal, Vallie. Everybody finished? Then we'd better get going. Office hours at Animal Inn begin in fifteen minutes."

"I'll put the dishes in the dishwasher," Val said. "Teddy, will you and Milton please feed the dogs? I've already given Cleveland his breakfast."

"I don't know anything about feeding dogs," Milton said.

"Here!" Teddy grabbed the dogs' dishes and shoved them at Milton. "It's no big deal. You hold 'em, I'll fill 'em." He began pouring dry dog food into the bowls.

"Is that what dogs eat?" Milton asked. "It looks like rocks to me."

"They like it," Teddy growled. "Dogs *like* rocks. And they *hate* orange marmalade."

Milton put the bowls on the floor, then stood with his hands sticking out. "May I wash my hands?" he asked. "There seems to be some old dog food stuck to the bowls. I'm afraid there could be germs on it."

"Wash your hands, Milton," Val sighed.

Milton did, scrubbing very carefully, and drying them thoroughly on a paper towel. Then he turned to Doc.

"Uncle Ted, I think I'd rather stay here and read a book. You don't really need me at Animal Inn, do you?"

"Oh, yes, we do, Milton," Doc said. "We need all the help we can get. You can read your book later. You'll like Animal Inn, and Vallie will introduce you to her horse, The Gray Ghost. You can ride him if you like. Do you know how to ride a horse?"

"Oh, yes," Milton said. "I've been taking riding lessons in Central Park for almost six months."

"Great! Vallie, Teddy, let's go."

"Right, Dad," Val sighed, and Teddy thrust his hands into the pockets of his jeans, scowling.

Suddenly he pulled out a battered envelope. "Hey, Milton, here's the letter I wrote you ages ago! I must have forgotten to send it."

Milton took the envelope. He opened it and read the letter.

"I don't collect baseball cards," he said. "I don't know much about sports. I'm sorry, Teddy. I guess I don't know much about anything you're interested in."

"That's okay," Teddy said gruffly. "It's not your fault you're a — "

"Everybody into the car *now*," Doc shouted.

"I'd really rather read my book," Milton murmured as he trotted after Teddy and Val.

It's a disaster, Val thought sadly. An honest to goodness, Grade-A-Number-One disaster!

Chapter 5

"Pat, I'd like you to meet my nephew, Milton," Doc said as they walked into Animal Inn's waiting room. "He's spending spring vacation with us. Milton, this is Pat Dempwolf, our receptionist."

"How do you do, ma'am," Milton said, gravely shaking Pat's hand.

"Well, aren't you the perfect little gentleman!" Pat cried.

"That's Milton, all right," Teddy muttered under his breath. Val poked him. "Well, he *is*," Teddy said.

"Where do you live, Milton?" Pat asked.

"In New York City," Milton replied.

"Erin's visiting our Aunt Peggy and Uncle John while Milton stays with us," Val added.

"Now isn't that nice! Aren't you lucky, Teddy, to have a little cousin to play with!" Pat beamed at both boys.

Teddy made no comment.

Pat bent down and rummaged in her pocket-book. When she straightened up, she held out two lollipops.

"One for each," she said. "But you mustn't eat them now. Save them for after lunch. I bought a bag of them for my little granddaughter, Tiffany. Tiffany just loves the cherry flavored ones."

"Thanks, Pat," Teddy said, taking one and shoving it into a pocket.

"Thank you very much, Mrs. Dempwolf," Milton said, "but I'm not allowed to eat sweets. My father says they rot your teeth."

"Oh." Pat looked a little disappointed, Val thought. "Well, maybe Vallie'd like it then."

"I sure would, Pat," Val said. She took the other lollipop. "Is Toby here yet?"

"Yes, he is. He's giving out morning medications. Why don't you take Milton into the infirmary and introduce him to Toby? Doc, these are your morning appointments. Charlie Tobias is coming at nine-fifteen for Scout's rabies shot. And Mrs. Bradley's Siamese. . . ."

"Come on, Milton. Let's say hello to Toby," Val said, leading the way to the infirmary.

"Who's Toby?" Milton asked.

"Toby's Doc's other assistant," Teddy said. "Toby Curran. His dad owns a real big dairy. Curran's ice cream is the best in the world." He narrowed his eyes. "Are you allowed to eat ice cream?"

"Yes," said Milton. "But only on special occasions, like birthdays. My father says — "

"I know," Teddy groaned. "It rots your teeth, right?"

"Only if you eat too much of it," said Milton.

They found Toby giving a pill to a long, thin cat. Val made the introductions.

"What's the matter with that cat?" Milton asked.

"Worms," Toby said cheerfully. "Real bad case. We thought old Tiger here was a goner, but he's gonna be all right now."

"Worms?" Milton repeated. Val thought he looked a little pale. "You mean — inside him?"

"Well, not *outside*," Toby said, grinning. "Cats and dogs get worms sometimes. But if you give them the right medicine, it zaps those worms, and the animal gets better right away. But if you don't, the animal starves to death 'cause the worms are eating all its food."

Milton turned paler.

"Hey, Milton, let's go see my horse," Val said quickly. "But first, I'll show you his trophy room."

Milton looked a little brighter. "Trophy room? Is he a champion?"

"He was," Teddy said. "He was a champion jumper when he was younger — he's pretty old now — older than Vallie. But he won lots of prizes."

"Is he . . . healthy?" Milton asked.

"Sure he is!" Val said. "He's as healthy as — as a horse! He's just old, like Teddy said. And he doesn't see very well, so he can't jump anymore. I bought him from the people who owned him. They were going to have him put to sleep because he couldn't win any more prizes."

"They were going to *kill* him?"

"They sure were," Toby put in. "That Mr. Merrill and his rotten daughter didn't care about The Ghost at all! But Val saved his life, and now he belongs to her."

Val proudly showed Milton the stall she and Toby had turned into a tack and trophy room for The Ghost. It wasn't really a trophy room, because Mr. Merrill hadn't given her the beautiful silver bowls and statues that The Ghost had won, but he had given her The Ghost's ribbons, and the blue and purple rosettes glowed in the dim light. She pointed out the newspaper clippings about The Ghost's triumphs, which Toby had framed, and several photographs of the big dapple-gray horse and his rider being awarded the trophies. The Ghost's saddle and bridle, gleaming with neatsfoot oil, were there, too.

"Gee!" Milton breathed. "He really *was* a champion!" He seemed really impressed.

"Better believe it," Teddy said.

"Now I'll let you meet him," Val said. "And

maybe later on today, you can ride him around the pasture."

"Me, too!" Teddy cried. "I can ride bareback," he told Milton. "Can you?"

"I never tried," said Milton. "But I'm afraid I won't be able to ride him at all."

"Sure, you will," Val said, leading the way to the barn where The Ghost was stabled. Doc's large animal patients had stalls there, too. "The Ghost's as gentle as a lamb."

"That's not the problem. I'm not allowed to go horseback riding without my hard hat," Milton said. "That's what my riding teacher said. If you're not wearing a hard hat, you might fall off and crack your skull."

"Gimme a break!" Teddy moaned.

"You could wear mine," Val offered. "It'll be a little big, I guess, but it's better than nothing."

"No, thank you, Vallie. If it doesn't fit, it won't protect me properly. I'll just pat him."

Toby said very quietly in Val's ear, "Is this kid for real? What does he think he is — a china doll or something?"

"That's just the way he is," Val sighed. "Okay, Milton. Here we are. Go ahead and pat him. Don't worry — he doesn't bite."

The Ghost greeted Val with whickers of pleasure. She threw her arms around his neck, then held his halter while Milton reached up to stroke him.

"He's a very handsome horse," Milton said. "I'm sorry I can't ride him."

"Guess I'll turn him loose in the pasture," Val said, after Teddy and Toby had said their hellos. "And then I'll have to go to work. Toby, why don't you show Teddy and Milton Mr. Fletcher's cow? Her mange is much better now — she'll be going home any day now."

"If it's all the same to you, Vallie, I don't think I want to see a mangy cow," Milton said politely. "Uncle Ted said he needed help. Do you have a job for me?"

"Uh . . ." Val thought very hard. What could she possibly give Milton and Teddy to do?

Toby came to her rescue. "You bet! Doc asked me to paint the fence out front, and it'll take me a week unless you and Teddy help me. Come on — I'll show you guys where the paint and brushes are."

Val breathed a sigh of relief, and led The Ghost out of his stall. As she took him out to the pasture, she heard Milton say, "May I wash my hands first? I smell all horsey."

Val rolled her eyes. She loved the smell of The Ghost. Erin had often teased her, saying that while other girls wore perfume that smelled like roses or violets, Val's favorite perfume was essence of horse. And Val had to admit she was right.

Well, at least Toby would keep the boys occupied while she worked with Doc. I owe you one, Toby, she thought gratefully.

"All right, Vallie, you can take Popcorn out to his master," Doc said two hours later.

Popcorn was a Checkered Giant rabbit with a bad case of ear mites. As Val lifted him off the examining table, she decided that he really *was* a giant. Popcorn weighed in at twelve pounds, more than twice what any of Val's rabbits — Flopsy, Mopsy, Cottontail, and Sam — weighed. But they were a different breed.

"Here you go, Ben," Val said, handing the huge, terrified animal to his teenage owner. She gave Ben a bottle of ear drops. "Put one drop in each ear three times a day. If the symptoms continue, give us a call. But I think Popcorn's going to be fine."

"Oh, Vallie, I have a phone message for you," Pat said after she had settled Ben's bill. "Mr. Pollard, the pig man, called. He said he'd stop in to see you around eleven-thirty."

Val checked her watch. It was almost eleven-thirty now. Why had Mr. Pollard called? It had to be because of Tiny. Maybe Tiny was *dying*! But if he was, Mr. Pollard would have called Doc, not Val.

"That's all he said? That he'd be here around eleven-thirty?" she asked.

"That's it. Is Doc ready for his next patient?"

"Yes . . . in a minute."

Val went to the front window and peered out, looking for Mr. Pollard's truck with the dancing pig painted on it. But all she saw were Toby, Teddy, and Milton slapping white paint on the fence.

Doc stuck his head out of the treatment room. "Next patient, please," he called.

"That's my Duke," said Mr. Ward, standing up. "*Heel*, Duke!"

The tiny chihuahua obediently moved next to Mr. Ward's foot and stood there, quivering all over. He wasn't nearly as big as Ben Rudisill's rabbit.

"Follow me, Mr. Ward," Val said after one last glance out the window.

What's wrong with Tiny? she wondered as she took Mr. Ward and Duke into the treatment room. The poor little piglet! If only she'd been able to take care of him, he'd have been strong and healthy by now.

When Duke had gotten his shots, Val came back out into the waiting room. And there sat Mr. Pollard with a big cardboard carton on his lap.

"Oh, Mr. Pollard, what's the matter with Tiny?" she cried. "It *is* Tiny, isn't it?"

"Sure is," said Mr. Pollard.

Val went over to him and looked into the carton. Tiny looked back at her from little piggy eyes fringed with long, pale lashes. He had a big blue ribbon around his neck, tied in a bow. He hadn't grown much since Val had last seen him, but he didn't look sick, either. And he wasn't coughing.

"Hi, little fella," Val said, stroking the piglet's back. "How you doing?"

Mr. Pollard answered for the piglet. "He's doing okay, but he won't be for long. His brothers and sisters just don't give him a chance. That's why I brought him to Animal Inn. He's yours, Vallie."

Val stared at him. *"Mine?"* she gasped.

"That's right. Mrs. Pollard and me been talking it over, and we figured that since you took such a shine to Tiny here, you ought to have him for your very own. He's a present, from us to you."

"Well, now, isn't that nice, Vallie," Pat said. "It's not every day somebody gets a pig for a present! Aren't you going to say thank you?"

"Oh, yes! Thank you, Mr. Pollard!"

Val picked the little pig up and cuddled him in her arms. Tiny grunted contentedly and poked Val's chin with his moist, pink snout.

"Nice pig," said Mrs. Stambaugh. She was waiting with her cat, Ruffles, to see Doc. "Kinda small though, ain't he?"

"Yep — runt of the litter," Mr. Pollard said. "Don't have time to fuss with him myself, so I'm giving him to Vallie, here."

"You take real good care of that pig, Vallie, and he'll fatten up just fine," Mrs. Stambaugh said. "You'll get a lot of prime pork from that little feller when he's grown."

Val shuddered. "Nobody's going to eat Tiny!" she cried.

Just then Doc came into the waiting room. "Ruffles can come in now, Vallie — " he began. He saw Tiny in Val's arms. "What's this little guy doing here? He's not sick again, is he?" he asked Mr. Pollard.

"Nope," Mr. Pollard replied. "Fit as a fiddle, Tiny is. I'm giving him to Vallie. That blue bow was the wife's idea, to make him look more like a present."

"Well, Luke, that's very nice of you, but — "

Mr. Pollard held up a hand. "Don't thank me, Doc. It's the least I can do. After all, you saved Sadie's whole litter." He stood up. "Well, I gotta be getting back to the farm. I'm just glad that Tiny has a good home."

As the door closed behind Mr. Pollard, Val said, "Dad, it wasn't my idea, honest. I know the rules about no new pets unless everybody agrees, but I didn't know how to say no."

"It's not your fault, Vallie," Doc said. Suddenly he began to laugh. "It looks as though we have a brand new pet, Duchess," he said.

"Duchess?" Val repeated.

"Remember *Alice in Wonderland*? When the

Duchess sprinkles pepper on the baby and it turns into a pig?"

Val laughed, too. "Of course I remember. Then I can keep him?" she asked hopefully.

"I don't think I have much choice," Doc said, still grinning.

"Super!" Val hugged Tiny so hard that he let out a little squeal. "Tiny Taylor, you're coming home with us!" she cried.

"Mrs. Stambaugh, I'm sorry to keep you waiting. Why don't you bring Ruffles in now?" Doc said. "Hairballs again, right?"

Mrs. Stambaugh picked up Ruffles' cat carrier and followed him into the treatment room. "You know how it is with long-haired cats, Doc. . . ."

Val was still snuggling Tiny when Toby, Teddy, and Milton trudged into the waiting room.

"We painted the whole fence," Toby said proudly. "Teddy and Milton did a great job. Teddy was faster, but Milton was neater."

"I wasn't all that neat," Milton said. "I got lots of paint on my pants. But not as much as Teddy!"

Teddy, whose blue jeans were now more white than blue, punched his cousin in the arm, but it was a friendly punch. "I gotta hand it to you, Milton. You're a pretty good worker."

Milton grinned. Val noticed that his horn-rimmed

glasses were spattered with tiny dots of paint, but he didn't seem to mind. "I've never painted before," Milton said. "If we need to have something painted, my parents hire people to do it. I *like* painting!"

Then he saw the pig.

"That's a cute pig," he said. "Is he sick?"

"Hey, Vallie, is that Tiny?" Teddy cried. "What's he doing here?"

"He's mine," Val said, beaming. "Mr. Pollard gave him to me, and Dad says I can keep him!"

"Wow" said Toby. "When he grows up, you'll have lots of pork chops and ham and sausage. . . ."

Val glared at him.

"Sorry, Val. I forgot you don't eat meat."

"I don't eat *pets*," Val said. "And Tiny's a pet. It would be like eating Cleveland or Jocko or Sunshine!"

Milton peered at Tiny through his paint-spattered glasses. "Pigs are very intelligent," he said. "I read about them in a book once. And some of my favorite stories are about Freddy, the pig detective. My father gave me all his Freddy the Pig books that he used to read when he was little."

"Pigs *are* intelligent," Val agreed. "They can learn all sorts of tricks."

"That's crazy," Teddy said. "Pigs are cute when they're little, like Tiny, but then they grow up to be big and dumb. I never heard of a pig that was as smart as a dog. Dogs can fetch and give you their paw and play dead and stuff like that. Whoever heard of a pig who could do that?"

"Freddy the pig detective solves all the mysteries at Mr. Bean's farm," Milton told him.

"But those are just stories! They're not real."

"No, they're not real, Teddy," Val said. "But pigs are smart. And I bet Tiny is a *very* smart pig."

"Oh, who cares!" Teddy grumbled. He looked at the clock behind the reception desk. "Hey, Vallie, Eric and Billy and Sparky are coming to the house at twelve-thirty for lunch — and to meet Milton. We're gonna play baseball after, in the empty lot behind Mr. Myers's house. Where's Dad? He has to drive Milton and me back home."

Val carefully put Tiny into his cardboard box.

"He's taking care of Ruffles Stambaugh's hairballs," she said. "He'll be through in a minute, and then he'll take you."

"What are hairballs?" Milton asked.

"Just what it sounds like," said Val. "Cats, particularly long-haired ones, get balls of hair in their stomachs because they wash themselves so much. Then they have to get medicine to dissolve the hairballs, or else they get real sick."

"That's disgusting," Milton said. "Don't you ever get tired of being around sick animals all the time?"

Before Val could answer, Toby said, "No, she doesn't, and neither do I. We like taking care of sick animals because it's so great when we can help them get better."

"I'm going to be a vet like Dad when I'm older," Val said. "Animals need doctors just like people do. We'd all be in pretty bad shape if nobody wanted to take care of sick *people*."

Milton thought about that. "I suppose you're right. I go to the doctor a lot — the eye doctor and the dentist and the pediatrician. I wonder if they ever get tired of *me*?"

"Not as long as your parents pay the bills!" Toby said.

Teddy paced back and forth impatiently. "I wish Dad would hurry up," he said.

"I don't mind waiting," Milton said. He sat down on one of the benches and picked up a copy of *Animal Health*. "I'll just sit here and read."

Toby gathered up the paint buckets and brushes and went off to clean the brushes. A few minutes later, Mrs. Stambaugh and Ruffles left, and Doc came out of the treatment room.

"Ready to go, boys?" he said.

"You bet!" cried Teddy, charging for the door.

"Milton, Dad's ready to go," Val said.

Milton looked up from his magazine. "Really?" He looked disappointed. "I was just reading a very interesting article about pigs. It's all about some pigs that have been taught to run races with each other. So pigs *are* smart. I kind of hoped I could finish reading it."

"Bring the magazine with you, Milton," Doc suggested. "You can finish it later, all right?"

"All right." Milton tucked the magazine under his arm. "Good-bye, Vallie." He leaned over Tiny's box. "Good-bye, Tiny. I never met a pig before, but you're a very nice one." Then he marched over to the reception desk. "Good-bye, Mrs. Dempwolf. It was a pleasure meeting you."

"Likewise, I'm sure," Pat said, smiling.

As Milton trotted after Doc, she turned to Val.

"I never met a little boy with such lovely manners! Imagine — he even said good-bye to your pig!"

"He's a perfect gentleman, like you said, Pat," Val said. "I just wish he'd loosen up a little. If anybody can make him relax and act like a normal kid, it's Teddy's gang." She gazed out the window, watching Milton climb into the car. "I bet by the time Dad and I come home tonight, Milton and Teddy will be real buddies!"

A grunt and a thud made her turn around. Tiny had gotten tired of sitting in the box and had knocked it over. Now the piglet began running all over the waiting room, his trotters slipping and sliding on the polished floor.

"Look at that pig travel!" Pat exclaimed. "Maybe he'll grow up to be one of those racing pigs your cousin Milton was talking about."

"I guess he needs exercise," Val said. "I know — I'll take him for a walk!"

She went over to the reception desk next to Pat and rummaged in the bottom drawer. At last she found what she was looking for — a collar and leash that had belonged to Jocko when he was a puppy.

She took off the big blue ribbon and replaced it with the collar. It fit Tiny's fat little neck perfectly. Val snapped on the leash and turned to Pat. "We're going out for a few minutes. You know, I bet I could teach him to heel, just like a dog, when he gets older."

"Now I've seen everything!" Pat cried, laughing. "A pig on a leash! My gracious!"

But Tiny sat down on his plump haunches and refused to budge when Val tugged gently on the leash. "Come on, Tiny," she coaxed. "We're going outside. It's a beautiful, warm spring day. The fresh air will do you lots of good."

She finally persuaded the piglet to stand up and take a few steps. She opened the door. Tiny raised his head and sniffed the air. Then suddenly he was off and running, with Val clutching the leash and dashing after him.

"Hey, speedy," she cried. "Wait for me!"

Chapter 6

"Well, Milton, did you have a good time with Teddy's friends?" Doc asked that evening as everyone sat down to supper. Val had served the excellent dinner Mrs. Racer had prepared. She'd already given Tiny his bottle, and the little pig was dozing in his cardboard box on the floor next to Val's chair. Cleveland was sitting on the kitchen counter, watching the sleeping piglet through narrowed yellow eyes, as though he knew that somewhere inside that small, pink body was a delicious pork chop.

"It was . . . very interesting," Milton replied, taking a forkful of peas.

"Interesting!" Teddy groaned. "Yeah, it was sure *interesting* when we were having our pizza, and Milton told us about the rat hairs! Sparky almost threw up."

"What rat hairs?" Val asked.

"In frozen pizza. In an article I read, I found out that they did a lot of tests on different kinds of frozen pizza, and some of them had rat hairs in them,"

Milton said calmly. "But I suppose the heat of the oven must kill most of the germs."

"And after that, it was *really* interesting when we were playing baseball, and Eric flied out to third. . . ."

"Flew," said Milton. "Not flied."

"He didn't flew, he *flied*!" Teddy yelled. "In baseball, it's *flied*! A fly ball flied out! Don't you know *anything*?"

"Teddy . . ." Doc warned.

But Teddy went right on. "So Eric flied out to third, and Milton was standing right there, and the ball was coming right at him, and he *ran away*! And Eric made a home run when he should have been out! So Eric's team won, and my team lost, just because Milton was afraid to try to catch the ball!"

"Oh, come on, Teddy," Val said. "It's not like you're talking about the World Series. It's no big deal."

Milton put down his fork. "I don't think I'm very hungry. I think I might be allergic to pot roast. May I please go to my room?"

"*Nobody* is allergic to pot roast, Milton," Doc said gently. "Maybe you'd rather have some of Vallie's vegetable casserole?"

Milton shook his head. "No, thank you. I don't feel very well. I'd really like to lie down."

Val looked at her father, and Doc nodded. "All

right, Milton. We'll call you when dessert is ready. Mrs. Racer made her special chocolate cake just for you."

"I break out in hives if I eat chocolate," Milton mumbled, pushing back his chair. His face looked pinched and pale. Nobody said anything as he hurried out of the kitchen.

Doc frowned at Teddy. "Teddy, you're behaving very badly. Instead of making your cousin feel at home, you're making him miserable."

"He's making *me* miserable!" Teddy said. "None of my friends want to come back while Milton's here. He's the wimpiest wimp in the world, Dad! I don't like him, and he doesn't like me. Can't you send him back to Aunt Peggy and Uncle John? That's what he wants, and that's what I want, too!"

"You're not being very nice to Milton," Val said. "Just because he's not good at the things you like to do doesn't give you the right to be nasty."

"I'm not being nasty! I just don't like him, that's all. I wish he wasn't my cousin! I just wish he'd go away!"

Teddy folded his arms on the butcher block table and rested his chin on them.

"Teddy, I think it's time we had a man-to-man talk about your cousin Milton," Doc said.

"Does that mean I'm excused?" Val asked. "Because if I am, I think I'll take up a glass of milk and some cookies to Milton. He hardly ate any dinner."

Teddy mumbled something she couldn't hear.

"What, Teddy?"

"I said you act like you like Milton better 'n me," he said, giving Val a sorrowful look.

"That's the silliest thing I ever heard!" Val said.

"No, it's not." Teddy blinked back tears. "Everybody treats him like he's a prince or something! Ever since Milton came here, I can't do anything right. You and Dad keep telling me to be nice to him, and Pat says what a little gentleman he is, and even Toby said he's a neater painter than I am."

"Oh, Teddy," Doc sighed. He put an arm around Teddy's shoulders. "Val's right. You're being silly. You know we don't like Milton better than you. We just want him to be comfortable and happy while he's staying with us, that's all."

"Doesn't anybody care if *I'm* comfortable and happy?" Teddy asked sadly.

"Indeed we do," said Doc. "We want you both to have a good time, but it's not working out that way. Got any ideas about how we can make it work better?"

"Well . . . I don't know . . ." Teddy began.

Val decided to let them talk in private. Tucking Tiny under one arm, and holding a plate in her other hand on which she had balanced a glass of milk, surrounded by some of Mrs. Racer's oatmeal-raisin cookies, she left the kitchen.

"Come on, Tiny. Let's go upstairs," she said.

When she reached the door of Erin's room, she tapped on it lightly with her foot.

"Can we come in?" she asked.

No answer. Val edged the door open a crack and peered in. She saw a small lump under the blankets of Erin's bed. The lump was quivering a little. Val thought she heard muffled sobs. Putting Tiny down on the floor, she went over to the bed and set the milk and cookies on the bedside table. Then she reached out and patted the lump.

"Milton, it's Vallie. I brought you a snack," she said.

The lump wriggled and heaved. Then Milton's head appeared. His hair was all mussed up, and his eyes were red and swollen.

"Th-thank you, Vallie," Milton croaked. He sniffled. "It's my allergies," he added, rubbing his eyes with his pajama sleeve. "I think I'm allergic to Dandelion."

The canary fluttered from perch to perch in his cage and gave an indignant trill.

"And I'm allergic to Jocko and Sunshine and Cleveland, too," Milton continued.

"I don't think so," Val said. She went over to Erin's dressing table, grabbed a wad of tissues, and brought them over to Milton. "Here — blow."

Milton blew.

"Are you allergic to milk and oatmeal cookies?" Val asked.

"I guess not," Milton said. He took a sip of the milk, then a bite of cookie.

Tiny, who had been exploring the room, came over to Val and huddled next to her feet, making sad little snuffling noises.

"What's the matter with Tiny?" Milton asked.

Val picked up the little pig and sat down on the bed. "I think he's homesick," she told Milton. "Even though his brothers and sisters weren't very nice to him, I guess he misses them anyway — and his mother, too. He's never been away from home before. He must feel awful lost and lonely."

"I guess he does," Milton said in a small, choked voice. "I bet he'd feel even worse if he'd had a really happy home, and then he went far away to stay with people he doesn't know at all. I bet he'd feel just terrible."

Two big, fat tears slid down Milton's flushed cheeks.

Val gave him another tissue. "I wouldn't be surprised if he developed a whole lot of allergies," she said solemnly.

Suddenly Milton turned away and curled up in a little ball.

"I'm not really allergic to everything," he confessed. Val could tell he was trying very hard not to cry.

"Maybe you're feeling a little homesick, too, just like Tiny," she said.

Milton nodded and swallowed a sob. "Everything's so different here," he said. "I'm not used to lots of animals and lots of strange people."

Val smiled. "We're not all that strange, not when you get to know us."

"You know what I mean — not strange like weird, strange like unfamiliar. I miss my mother and my father and my friends." Milton gulped. "I even miss the doorman of my apartment building! I'm sorry, Vallie. You and Uncle Ted are trying real hard to like me, I can tell. But Teddy. . . ."

"Stop right there!" Val said. "We're not *trying* to like you, Milton. We *do* like you."

"Teddy doesn't, and neither do his friends. They think I'm clumsy and a coward and stuckup — they *do*," he insisted before Val had a chance to speak. "I heard that girl Sparky telling Teddy so. And *he* thinks I'm a wimp. I can't help it if I don't know how to play baseball. I've never been good at sports. I'd rather read, or play computer games. I just want to go home!"

He buried his face in the pillow, his shoulders shaking with sobs.

Val patted his back, not knowing what else to do.

"Psst! Vallie!"

A whisper from the doorway made her look up. Teddy was standing there. Val shook her head and motioned for him to go away, but he didn't.

"Dad says I have to apologize," Teddy said, coming slowly into the room. "So here I am."

Milton turned around. "Now you can call me a crybaby, too," he said. "Well, I don't care. I'm not like you, Teddy. I guess I'm just about as different from you as a person can be, but there's nothing I can do about it."

Teddy scuffed at the rug with the toe of one sneaker. "Look, Milton, I'm sorry about today. It's not your fault you're a wimp." (Val groaned.) "I should've known you wouldn't like playing baseball — I should've asked you what *you'd* like to do instead. Tomorrow we'll do whatever you want, okay? You name it, we'll do it."

Milton swallowed. "That's very nice of you, Teddy. I — I can't think of anything right now." He brightened a little. "Unless you'd like me to teach you how to play computer chess. It's really fun."

Teddy shrugged. "Sure, if that's what you want." He didn't look very enthusiastic, Val noticed. Milton noticed, too, and his face fell. Neither of them seemed to have any more suggestions.

Oh, dear, Val thought, absently tickling Tiny under the chin. If somebody doesn't think of something fast, Milton's going to start crying again, and Teddy'll be gloomy, too. What a vacation this is turning out to be!

She tried desperately to remember something — anything — that Milton had been enthusiastic about besides computer chess. He'd liked painting the fence, but that was all done. And he'd liked The Ghost, but he wouldn't ride without his hard hat. . . .

Suddenly her eye fell on the copy of *Animal Health* that Milton had brought back from Animal Inn. On the cover was a picture of the racing pigs Milton had been reading about. He'd been very interested in that, and in Tiny.

"You know, guys," she said casually, "I have kind of a problem with Tiny here."

"What do you mean, a problem?" Teddy asked.

"Well, like I was telling Milton, Tiny's really lonely and homesick without his family. And he's going to be a lot lonelier when I'm not here to take care of him."

"You mean because you're going to be working with Uncle Ted at Animal Inn?" Milton asked. "Can't you take Tiny with you?"

"Yes, I could, but it won't be any better there," Val said with a sigh. "I'll be so busy that I won't have time to play with him and make him feel at home.

And after work tomorrow, I'm going over to Jill's house — Jill's my best friend," she explained to Milton. "I hate to think of poor Tiny sitting around all day, feeling sadder and sadder. Maybe I ought to call Mr. Pollard and tell him I can't keep Tiny, and ask him to take him back."

"But you said his brothers and sisters weren't very nice to him," Milton said.

"Yeah, Vallie. And what if his mother rolls over on him and *smothers* him to death?" Teddy added. "You can't give him back to Mr. Pollard."

"*Smothers* him? That's terrible!" Milton cried.

"Yes, it is," Val said sadly. "But I don't know what else to do." She looked down at the piglet nestled in her arms. "Poor Tiny! I'd really like to keep you, but unless I can find you a baby-sitter — or two . . ." she glanced from Teddy to Milton ". . . I guess it's back to the pig farm. If you survive there, then you'll be turned into another Pollard Pork Product."

Milton sat straight up in bed. He groped on the bedside table for his glasses and carefully put them on. "You can't let that happen to him," he said. "Tiny's such a nice little pig. You can't let him be smothered or grow up and be butchered!"

"Hey, I have a great idea!" Teddy said. Milton and me don't have any plans for tomorrow — right, Milton?"

Milton nodded.

"Why don't we take care of Tiny for you?" Teddy asked eagerly. "We could give him his bottle, and play with him so he doesn't get lonely."

"And I could teach him some tricks," Milton added. "Like it says in that magazine article, pigs are very intelligent."

Teddy scowled. "You're wrong. Pigs are dumb."

"*You're* wrong. They're smart!" Milton said.

"Well, if pigs are smart and *you're* so smart, then go ahead — try to teach him some tricks. Betcha can't!"

"Bet I can!"

"Can't!"

"Can!"

Val grinned. "Why don't we find out? Milton, you're going to be here for eight more days. Think you can teach Tiny some tricks before you go back to New York?"

"I'm sure I can," Milton said. Then his face fell. "But that article said that those pigs learned to race because they loved the rewards they got at the end, like chocolate chip cookies. And Tiny only drinks milk."

"He's old enough to be weaned," Val said quickly. "You and Teddy could help me wean him. Try him out with one of those oatmeal-raisin cookies."

Milton picked up a cookie from the bedside table and held it under Tiny's nose. Val, Milton, and Teddy watched as Tiny snuffled at the cookie. When the piglet took a very small bite, they all broke out in smiles.

"He likes it!" Teddy cried.

"Naturally," said Val. "Mrs. Racer makes the best oatmeal-raisin cookies in the world."

"You're feeding Mrs. Racer's cookies to a *pig*?" Doc said. Nobody had seen him come into the room. Now he came over to the side of Milton's bed. "Well, look at that! The little fellow really does seem to like it."

"Uncle Ted, Teddy and I are going to baby-sit for Tiny tomorrow," Milton said eagerly. "And I'm going to start to teach him some tricks!"

"*We're* going to teach him some tricks," Teddy said. "Milton said he could teach him all by himself, but he doesn't know anything about animals, so I guess I better help him."

"What a good idea!" Doc said. He met Val's eyes and winked. Val winked back. "Tell you what," he said. "If you can get this piglet to learn three tricks by the time Milton goes back to New York, I'll take everybody to Curran's Dairy Store, and buy all the ice cream each of you can eat."

"Just as long as it's not chocolate," Milton said. "I really *am* allergic to chocolate."

"*I'm* not," Teddy said.

"Neither am I!" said Val.

Milton held out another cookie. "Here, Tiny. Want another bite?"

Tiny grunted and struggled out of Val's arms to nibble at the cookie.

Milton giggled. "Wait till I tell my parents that I had a *pig* on my bed! They won't believe it!"

Val was the first one to hear the telephone ring.

"I'll get it!" she shouted, leaving Tiny munching his cookie. She dashed into the hall and picked up the phone.

"Vallie! It's me, Erin!"

"Erin!" Val cried. "How's it going? Are you having a good time?"

"The very best time of my entire life!" Erin crowed. "New York City is the most wonderful place in the world, and we're going to the New York City Ballet at Lincoln Center tonight! Today, Aunt Peggy took me up and down Fifth Avenue. We saw all the fancy stores, like Saks and Lord & Taylor and Tiffany's, and we had lunch in Rockefeller Center! Oh, Vallie, I wish you were here with me! Let me talk to Daddy."

"Dad, it's Erin, and she wants to talk to you," Val said, holding out the receiver to Doc. As he began to talk to Erin, Val went back into her sister's room where Milton and Teddy were playing with Tiny.

"Is she calling from home?" Milton asked. "May I speak to my parents?"

He hopped out of bed and padded over to Doc in the hall. When Doc handed the phone to him, he said, "Mother? It's me, Milton. Guess what! There's a *pig* on my bed! His name is Tiny, because he's so little, and Teddy and I are going to take care of him while Vallie's working . . . Yes, Mother, he is a very clean pig . . . Yes, I brush my teeth three times a day . . . Yes, I'm taking my allergy pills, and my vitamins . . . Yes, everything is fine. Yes, I miss you, too. It's very different, but it's . . ." he looked at Teddy, who was standing in the doorway of Erin's room. ". . . it's okay. Really, it is! See you next week."

Thank goodness! Val thought. Maybe it's going to work out all right after all.

Chapter 7

But when Val got up the next morning, she had second thoughts about leaving Tiny with his two "baby-sitters." Neither Teddy nor Milton knew anything at all about pigs, much less about baby pigs. What if they wore him out playing with him? What if Teddy was too rough, and Tiny got hurt?

Val knelt next to Tiny's carton. She'd folded an old, soft towel on the bottom to make him a cozy bed, and underneath the towel she'd placed an electric heating pad turned on low so he'd be nice and warm. Tiny grunted and snuffled excitedly when she reached in to pat him. He immediately began sucking on one of her fingers.

"Hungry, huh?" Val said, laughing. "Well, you'll just have to wait a few minutes till I get dressed. Then we'll go downstairs and have breakfast. I'm going to fix you some nice warm mash. It won't taste as good as Mrs. Racer's cookies, but I bet you'll like it."

Cleveland had been sleeping on Val's bed, as he always did. Now he yawned, stretched, and jumped down onto the floor next to Tiny's box. The big orange cat stood on his hind legs, resting his front paws on the edge of the carton. His pink nose met Tiny's snout, and the two animals sniffed each other warily. Cleveland was every bit as big as the piglet — bigger, if you counted Cleveland's long, fat tail.

Suddenly Tiny lunged for the cat, knocking over the box. Cleveland ran for the door, Tiny at his heels. Val barely grabbed Tiny in time to stop him from running after Cleveland down the hall. The piglet squealed and struggled in her arms, waving all four pink trotters in the air.

"Take it easy, Tiny," Val said. Small as he was, she was having a hard time holding him. "Guess you're not as weak as I thought!"

"What's all the racket?" Doc came out of his room in his pajamas, looking sleepy.

"Was that Tiny?" Teddy asked, poking his head out his door, followed by Jocko, who had, as usual, spent the night under his bed.

"Pigs certainly have loud voices," Milton added as he came into the hall.

"Everything's okay," Val assured them. By now Tiny had calmed down and was resting innocently in Val's arms.

Doc yawned and stretched. "Just what this house needs — an alarm pig." He shuffled down the hall in his bare feet to the bathroom. "Be out in a minute."

Teddy wandered out of his room, his eyes still heavy with sleep. He patted the piglet's head. "Morning, Tiny," he said. Val noticed that he was holding Fuzzy-Wuzzy by one moth-eaten leg.

Milton noticed, too. "That's a very nice bear," he said.

Teddy froze. Suddenly wide awake, he hid Fuzzy-Wuzzy behind his back. "What bear?" he asked weakly.

"May I see him?" Milton asked.

"No!" Teddy's face turned beet red. He started backing into his room.

Val knew how Teddy must be feeling. The fact that he still slept with a stuffed toy was a deep, dark secret from everyone outside the family. Teddy had made Val and Erin promise they'd never tell any of his friends because he was sure they'd laugh at him.

"Teddy, wait! Don't go away!" Milton cried. He dashed into Erin's room. A moment later he came back, clutching a bedraggled stuffed rabbit. The rabbit wasn't in much better shape than Fuzzy-Wuzzy, and one of its eyes was missing.

Teddy had vanished into his room, closing the door behind him. Milton knocked politely.

"Will you please open the door?" he asked. "I want to show you something."

"Open up, Teddy," Val urged.

No response.

"Teddy Taylor, you open that door right now!" she shouted.

The door opened just a crack.

"What?"

Milton pushed the door open all the way.

"This is Roscoe," Milton said, shoving the rabbit at Teddy. "I've had him ever since I can remember. I can't sleep unless I've got Roscoe. I didn't want you to know about him, because I was afraid you'd make fun of me." He smiled shyly.

"When I was little, I used to sleep with Fuzzy-Wuzzy," Val put in. "And then I passed him on to Erin, and she passed him on to Teddy."

Teddy stood in the open doorway. He looked from Milton to Val. Then very slowly he brought Fuzzy-Wuzzy from behind his back. "I won't make fun of you if you won't make fun of *me*," he said to Milton.

"Cross my heart and hope to die," Milton said solemnly.

The two little boys stared at each other for a minute. At last Teddy said, "Okay. I wouldn't fink on a member of my very own family."

"Me, neither!" Milton said happily.

Val squeezed Tiny so hard that the piglet let out an indignant squeal. "All *right*!" she cried. "That's the way cousins ought to talk! Breakfast will be ready in about half an hour, soon as I get dressed."

Milton started back to Erin's room. "Vallie," he said as he passed her, "if it's all right with you, I'd just as soon not have bacon this morning." He glanced at Tiny. "I don't think I'll ever eat bacon again."

"Me, neither!" said Teddy.

Val beamed. "That's fine by me. How about granola and some nice fresh fruit?"

"Sounds good to me," Teddy said, swinging Fuzzy-Wuzzy by one leg.

"Me, too," Milton agreed, holding Roscoe close.

"Next!" said Doc as he came out of the bathroom.

"My turn!"

Val dumped Tiny in her room and ran down the hall.

"Me and Milton'll go after you, Vallie," Teddy said.

"But what are you going to do with Tiny when he grows up?" Jill Dearborne asked Val later that afternoon. The two girls had just come back to Jill's house after seeing a movie at the Capital, the only theatre in town. Now they were drinking soda and waiting for the popcorn to be ready that Jill had put in the popper.

"I haven't thought about that yet," Val admitted. "I was just so surprised when Mr. Pollard gave him to me — and when Dad let me keep him — that I didn't think ahead at all."

Jill took the butter she'd been melting off the stove. "When he's big and fat, I bet Mr. Pollard would take him back," she said.

"Oh, sure he would. He'd take him back and turn him into more Pollard Pork Products," Val said. "No way! I have to find a place for him where he'll be treated like a pet, not run through a meat grinder and packed into sausage skins."

"That's a pretty gruesome thought, all right." Jill turned off the popper. "Popcorn's ready." She took off the lid and poured on the melted butter. "Here — have some."

"Mmm, this is great!" Val mumbled through a mouthful of warm popcorn. "I was thinking about Wildlife Farm. They took Gigi and Little Leo. Maybe they'd be interested in adding a pig to their petting zoo."

"Maybe," Jill agreed. "But a monkey and a lion cub are kind of special, and a pig's — well, a pig's just a pig, know what I mean?"

"Not Tiny. Tiny's different. He's really smart, I can tell."

"Come on, Val. He's just a baby. How can you tell he's smart?" Jill asked.

"I just know, that's all." Val said stubbornly.

"Teddy and Milton are going to try to teach him some tricks. I bet he learns real fast."

"What kind of tricks? Like dog tricks — sit up, roll over, play dead?"

"Search me," Val replied. "Pigs are just as smart as dogs, maybe even smarter. And if Tiny learns a few simple tricks, he'd be a *very* special pig, and Wildlife Farm would take him in a minute."

"Okay — I've heard enough about Tiny the Wonder Pig," Jill said. "Tell me about your little cousin. Are Milton and Teddy getting along all right?"

"Well. . . ." Val hesitated. "Yes and no. Or maybe I ought to say no and yes."

"What does that mean?"

"It means I'm not sure. The past two days were pretty awful. Milton's as different from Teddy as he could possibly be. He's more like a robot than a kid! He has perfect manners, and he's not interested in sports, and he reads all the time, and he's allergic to stuff, and . . . well, he's an only child, so I guess that explains it."

Jill gave her a dirty look. "Thanks a bunch! I'm an only child, too, remember. Do I act like a robot?"

Val giggled. "Only sometimes!"

Jill threw a piece of popcorn at her, which Val deftly caught and put in her mouth. "Just kidding," she said. "But Milton's a *big city* only child. He lives in a big apartment building — he can't run outside and play like a normal kid. He has to wait for the elevator, and then somebody has to take him wherever he wants to go. And the really weird part of it is, he *likes* it! He's awfully homesick. Last night he cried a lot. He misses Aunt Peggy and Uncle John. He even misses the doorman of his apartment building!"

"Sounds weird, all right," Jill agreed. "So it's a real disaster, huh?"

"Yes and no," Val said again. "Last night, it looked like the only thing to do with old Milton was put him on the next train for New York City. But then I got this idea that maybe Milton and Teddy could take care of Tiny today while I was gone. Milton kind of liked Tiny the first time he met him, and he knows how intelligent pigs are. So Teddy bet Milton he couldn't teach Tiny some tricks, and Milton took the bet. And this morning, the guys seemed to be getting along a little better. But I haven't checked in with them all day." She looked at the kitchen clock. "I hope everything's okay."

"Mrs. Racer's been there, hasn't she?" Jill asked. Val nodded. "Then they're okay. Hey, let's go to your house and see how everything's going!" Jill suggested. "That is, if you can tear yourself away from my terrific popcorn."

Val scooped up the last few fluffy white morsels. "I *have* been pigging out, haven't I? Guess it's Tiny's influence. That's a good idea, Jill. But I'd better wash my hands first. I'm all buttery."

A few minutes later, the girls were biking down the street to the Taylor's big stone house on Old Mill Road. The weather was warm and sunny. Forsythia bushes were blooming in every yard, and tulips and hyacinths brightened the gardens of the houses they passed. How could Milton not like being in Essex? Val wondered. She was sure there was nothing as pretty in New York City. I never want to live anywhere else, she thought, as the sweet spring breeze blew through her hair.

As she turned into the driveway of the Taylors' house, her heart sank. She saw Milton, running at top speed, with Teddy in hot pursuit. She braked to a stop just as Teddy caught up with Milton and tackled him, flinging him to the ground. Milton's glasses flew off and landed a few feet in front of her bike.

"Gotcha!" Teddy yelled.

"Teddy!" Val hollered at the top of her lungs. 'Leave your little cousin alone!" She leaped off her bike and ran over to the two boys. "Milton, are you okay?"

She'd expected to see tears streaming down Milton's face. Instead, he grinned up at her. "I'm fine, Vallie. Teddy's been teaching me how to play touch football, and I just made a home run!"

"A *touchdown*, dummy!" Teddy shouted. "Don't you know *anything*?"

Milton struggled to his feet, clutching Teddy's football to his chest. His hair was standing on end, and his shirt was covered with mud. There was a rip in his carefully pressed blue jeans. Jocko and Sunshine galloped over to him, jumping up and licking his face.

"Cut that out!" Milton yelled. "Hey, Ted, let's do it again! You take the ball this time."

He tossed the football at Teddy, who caught it and tucked it under his arm.

"Okay! C' mon, Milt — this time you can tackle *me*!"

The dogs were barking loudly, leaping up on Val, and Jill, who had just parked her bike.

"Who're you?" Milton asked, squinting at Jill.

"This is my best friend, Jill Dearborne," Val said. "Jill, this is our cousin Milton."

"Hi, Milton," Jill said.

"Call me Milt," Milton said, sticking out a grubby hand. "Milt the Stilt — that's what Teddy calls me. There's a basketball player who used to be called Wilt the Stilt because he was so tall. I'm not very tall, and I don't know how to play basketball, but I'll grow."

Val picked up Milton's glasses and handed them to him.

"Thanks, Vallie." Milton placed them carefully on his nose. "You're not very tall, either," he said to Jill.

"That's Jill the Pill," Teddy said, tossing the football at Jill. "She's like another sister. I have more sisters than I know what to do with!"

"And I have more *brothers* than I know what to do with!" Val said, laughing and tickling Teddy in the ribs.

"You only have one brother," Teddy giggled.

"I know! But that's more than I know what to do with!" Val let Teddy go, and grinned at Jill.

Milton hitched up his jeans — and saw the rip over his knee. "Oops, I tore my pants." He looked worried for a moment, then a big grin spread over his face. "But Mrs. Racer can fix them, right, Teddy?"

"Better believe it," Teddy said. "C'mon, Milt — we gotta feed the rabbits and my chickens and Vallie's dumb duck."

"Archie is *not* a dumb duck!" Val said indignantly. "And where's Tiny? I thought you two were going to try to teach him some tricks."

"We started," Milton told her. "We're working on teaching him how to shake hands. He almost got it, didn't he, Ted?"

"Almost," Teddy said. "We got him to pick up his front paw when we said 'paw' and held out one of Mrs. Racer's cookies."

"Trotter," Val said. "A pig's foot is called a trotter."

"But Tiny doesn't know what it's called," Teddy said. "We're teaching him 'paw,' so he thinks he has paws. That's the way we taught Jocko."

"Let's go feed those animals," Milton said. " 'Bye, Vallie. 'Bye, Jill. Could I have the football back?"

"Be my guest," Jill said, throwing the football to Milton.

"Hey, you caught it!" Teddy cried. "You're getting better, Milt."

"I'm trying," Milton said, trotting after Teddy toward the garage where the rabbits, the chickens, and the duck had their pens.

"I don't know what you were talking about, Val," Jill said, watching the two little boys as they ran off. "Milton looks pretty normal to me."

"Yeah, he does, doesn't he?" Val said.

Teddy and Milton disappeared into the garage, followed by Jocko and Sunshine.

"Let's go and see how Mrs. Racer and Tiny are getting along," Val suggested.

"I wonder how she feels about having a pig running around the house," Jill mused.

Chapter 8

Val and Jill entered the house through the back door which led into the kitchen. Val immediately smelled something delicious.

"Hi, Mrs. Racer. What're you baking?" she asked.

"Hello, Vallie, Jill. Oatmeal-raisin cookies, that's what."

Mrs. Racer bent down and slid a cookie sheet into the oven.

"There's a pile of 'em on that plate over there." She pointed to the butcher block table. "All I can say is, better eat 'em fast before that little piglet does!"

Val and Jill each helped themselves to a cookie. "Tiny's really crazy about those cookies, isn't he?" Val said.

"He sure is. Never seen a little pig take to solid food so quick. I keep telling Teddy and Milton not to feed him so much, but every time my back is turned, there's another cookie or two missing, and that pig's got crumbs all over his snout."

"Where is Tiny, anyway?" Val wanted to know. "Jill hasn't seen him yet."

"Probably in the dining room, under the table," Mrs. Racer said. "Teddy and Milton put him there when they went out." She shook her white head. "It's not natural, having a pig in the house, and that's the truth. Not that Tiny's not a real clean pig, mind you, but he's a pig nevertheless, and pigs belong in pens, not in respectable people's dining rooms."

"I know, Mrs. Racer," Val said, "but I was afraid he'd be lonely and cold if we left him at Animal Inn."

She and Jill went into the dining room. Val got down on her knees and stuck her head between two of the chairs. There was Tiny, all right, sound asleep. His tummy looked much fatter than it had that morning.

Val poked him where she knew his ribs should be, though she couldn't see them. "Wake up, Tiny. Say hello to Jill."

The piglet quivered and opened his eyes, letting out a startled grunt.

Jill giggled. "Look at that! When he was asleep, his tail was straight as a string, but the minute he woke up, it curled! He's a cute pig!"

Val gently took Tiny's front legs and pulled him out from under the table. "Come on, Tiny. Let's see your trick," she said.

"And that's another thing," said Mrs. Racer from

the kitchen doorway. "It's not natural, teaching pigs to do tricks like they was circus animals. But try to tell that to Teddy and Milton! No wonder the poor little thing is all wore out. They've been pestering the life out of him, teaching him to shake hands. And every time he does, they give him another cookie. He's going to get a bellyache, just you wait and see."

"Can I try to make him do it just once?" Val pleaded. "Just once, that's all. And only one cookie, I promise."

"Guess one more won't do him any harm, seeing how many he's had already," sighed Mrs. Racer.

Jill went into the kitchen and came back with a cookie. She gave it to Val. "I just *love* coming to your house, Val," she said. "There's always something interesting going on!"

Val sat Tiny down and held the cookie in front of his little pink snout. "Okay, Tiny, do your stuff. *Paw.*"

Tiny lunged for the cookie, but Val firmly sat him back down.

"Not until you shake hands," she said. "Come on, Tiny. *Paw!*"

This time the piglet wriggled, snuffled, grunted, and rolled over on his back.

"No, no," Val sighed. She picked him up and plopped him into a sitting position once more. Holding the cookie just out of reach, she repeated, *"Paw!"*

Tiny looked from Val to the cookie and back again. Then he lifted his right front trotter slowly, about an inch from the floor. Val grabbed it and shook it enthusiastically.

"That's the way!" she cried. "Boy, are you ever a smart pig!"

She gave him the cookie, and Tiny gobbled it up in two seconds flat. He was so happy that his tail curled into a perfect corkscrew shape.

"He's smart, all right," Jill said, impressed. "He's about the smartest pig I ever saw! Come to think of it, he's about the *only* pig I ever saw, close up."

"It's not natural," Mrs. Racer grumbled. "Pigs weren't meant to do circus tricks."

Val sat back on her heels, looking up at Mrs. Racer.

"Maybe not, but they can *learn*. I think it's neat that Teddy and Milton taught him to do this in just one day."

Mrs. Racer went back into the kitchen to take a tray of cookies out of the oven.

"Maybe," she said, lifting each cookie with a spatula and putting them on the marble counter. "But what good's it going to do Tiny? That's what I want to know. Say he learns a whole lot of tricks. Where's he going to end up — in a carnival like the one where you found that poor, sick monkey and the lion cub?"

"Val says maybe Wildlife Farm would take him," Jill put in.

Val had followed them into the kitchen, Tiny in her arms. "He'd be real popular at Wildlife Farm. The little kids would love him."

"Pigs belong on *real* farms," Mrs. Racer said again. "That's where *this* pig would be happy. On a farm, with others of his own kind."

"But Mrs. Racer," Val said, "if he goes to a farm, he'll wind up being *butchered*! I can't let that happen to Tiny!"

Mrs. Racer turned back to the oven, putting in four Idaho potatoes. She muttered something that Val couldn't hear.

"What did you say, Mrs. Racer?" she asked.

Mrs. Racer turned to face her. "I said, not on *my* farm."

Tiny was struggling to get down. Val lowered him to the floor. "*Your* farm?" she echoed.

"That's right." Mrs. Racer smoothed down her spotless apron. "I'd take that little pig, let him live a normal pig life. I got a few pigs — some chickens, and some cows, too. M'son Henry raises chickens for market. He wouldn't take to a pig. But I could take Tiny. Wouldn't matter to me if he did tricks or not. I wouldn't butcher him, Vallie. I know how you feel about things like that. I'd take real good care of him."

Val ran to Mrs. Racer and threw her arms around her waist.

"*Would* you? Would you give Tiny a home?"

Mrs. Racer gave Val a big hug.

"Indeed I would. Those tricks Teddy and Milton are teaching him won't do him much good, but I guess they won't do him any harm, either. From what I've seen today, those boys are learning more than the pig is! Milton's come out of himself something wonderful, and Teddy's having a good time, too. By the time Milton goes back to New York City, he and Teddy will be real good friends, and that little pig has a lot to do with it." She reached up and smoothed a strand of Val's hair back from her forehead. "So I guess he deserves a home where nobody'll do him any harm, and where he won't have to perform for folks like he was a freak in a side show. Once Milton goes home, I'll take Tiny. M'son Henry can pick him up one night when he stops by for me." She gave Val a little pat and released her. "M'son Henry's probably gonna think I've gone plumb crazy, taking in a pig that won't ever wind up in the smokehouse! But I can handle him. He's a good boy, m'son Henry is."

"Oh, Mrs. Racer, thank you!" Val cried happily.

"I can't think of anywhere I'd rather have Tiny live. Isn't that great, Jill?"

"It sure is," Jill agreed. She grinned at Mrs. Racer. "Will you keep on baking oatmeal-raisin cookies for him?"

Mrs. Racer pretended to scowl. "I will not! Wasn't baking 'em for him in the first place. No, sir, when Tiny's at my place, he's gonna live like a normal pig and eat what the other pigs eat. And he'll like it, you'll see. Like I said, pigs are pigs. They'll eat anything you feed 'em."

She looked down at Tiny, who was sitting at her feet, snuffling, and grunting. It seemed to Val that the piglet was smiling. He lifted his right front trotter hopefully.

"Well, will you just look at that little beggar!" said Mrs. Racer, trying very hard not to smile back at Tiny. "Want another cookie, do you?" She took one from the latest batch and offered it to him. Tiny gobbled it up.

"My lands!" Mrs. Racer sighed. "That pig's worse than a dog! If he gets sick, it's his own fault." She glanced up and met Val's amused gaze. "Well, it's *mostly* his own fault. That little feller's too cute for his own good!"

The kitchen door burst open, and Teddy and Milton ran in, followed by Jocko and Sunshine.

"Guess what, Mrs. Racer?" Milton said, skidding to a stop by the kitchen counter. "Teddy let me feed the rabbits, and Archie, too, and I picked up one of the rabbits — which one was it, Teddy?"

"Cottontail," Teddy said, grabbing a cookie and stuffing it into his mouth.

"That's right — Cottontail. Teddy says Cottontail usually scratches, but he didn't scratch *me*! And you know what I think? *I* think those rabbits would like some carrots. Do we have any carrots in the refrigerator?"

"Lots," said Val. "They're in the vegetable crisper. Why don't you get some and take them out to the rabbits?"

Milton hesitated. "May I have some carrots, Mrs. Racer?"

Mrs. Racer opened the refrigerator door. "Take as many as you like, Milton. But then I want you all to clear out of my kitchen. How do you expect me to fix your supper when you're all over the place, getting into everything? Teddy Taylor, *no more cookies*! Vallie, take that pig out of here right now. Jill, Cleveland wants to go outside . . . *Cleveland*!" She swatted at the big orange cat, who had just leaped up onto the counter and was delicately sniffing at the cookies. "There won't be any left for Doc when he gets home, what with pigs and cats and children eating everything in sight!"

Jill scooped Cleveland up and headed for the

back door. Val tucked Tiny under her arm and took him into the dining room. Teddy grabbed a handful of lettuce from the crisper and hurried after Milton, shouting, "Hey Milt the Stilt, wait up!"

When Jill came back in, she joined Val and Tiny in the living room. The piglet was stretched out in front of the TV, grunting ecstatically as Val rubbed his fat little stomach. Jill plopped down beside them.

"You're a lucky pig, Tiny," she said, scratching Tiny behind the ears. "You're going to be just fine."

"He *is* a lucky pig," Val said. "He brought us luck, too. If it wasn't for Tiny, Milton would still be a wimp, and Teddy would still be miserable."

"You've been lucky for him, too," Jill pointed out. "Now he'll never be a Pollard Pork Product!"

Val smiled down at the little pig. Tiny definitely smiled back.

By the time Milton's visit came to an end, he and Teddy had taught Tiny three tricks. The piglet had learned to lie down and to roll over, besides offering his right front trotter. True to his word, Doc took them all to Curran's Dairy Store for all the ice cream they could eat. Val was amazed at the amount of raspberry, strawberry, and butter pecan that Milton was able to put away.

And now Val, Doc, Teddy, and Mrs. Racer were

waiting with Milton at the Harrisburg railroad station for the train that would carry him back to New York. Milton looked exactly as he had when he'd arrived — navy blue blazer, neatly pressed gray slacks, button-down shirt, and striped tie — but he was a very different Milton inside.

"Wait till I tell my friends that my cousins had a *pig* living in their house, and we taught it to do tricks, just like a dog!" he said excitedly. "And that I learned to play football, and went fishing even though I didn't catch anything, and I took care of rabbits and chickens and ducks, and. . . ."

"Uh, Milton, maybe you'd better not mention the part about the pig living in the house," Doc said quickly. "Somehow I don't think your parents would be exactly thrilled by the idea."

"Oh, it's okay, Uncle Ted. I already told them on the phone," Milton said. "Mother said it was very unusual. She wanted to know if Tiny was housebroken, and I told her yes." He turned to Teddy. "I can't wait to come visit you again this summer. I'll bring my hard hat so I can ride The Ghost."

"And when I come to visit *you*," Teddy said, "we'll go to the zoo, and we'll play computer chess, and. . . ."

"And I'll get my father to take us to Shea Stadium so we can see a baseball game. Maybe the Yankees will be playing the Phils."

"The Yankees don't play at Shea," Teddy said patiently. "The Mets do."

"Oh — sorry. I guess I'll have to do a lot of reading before I know as much about sports as you do," said Milton.

"Yeah, you probably will," Teddy agreed.

Val moved closer to the edge of the platform and cocked an ear. "I think I hear the train coming," she said.

"Well, Milton, how about giving your Uncle Ted a hug?" said Doc. "It's been a real pleasure having you stay with us."

Milton flung his arms around Doc's waist and hugged him hard.

"Thank you for everything, Uncle Ted," he said. "And you know what? I'm going to tell my father I think he ought to grow a beard just like yours. It's very distinguished-looking."

"Distinguished-looking, eh?" Doc repeated, trying very hard to keep a straight face. "Thank you very much, Milton. Nobody's ever described me in quite that way before."

The train was in sight now, purring down the track.

"Good-bye, Vallie," Milton said, sticking out a hand for her to shake. "I really like all your animals. I bet you'll be a wonderful vet some day, just like Uncle Ted."

"I'm going to try," Val said, ignoring the hand. "If you don't mind too much, I'd like to kiss you good-bye. Teddy lets me kiss him sometimes, even though he says kissing's icky."

"It *is* icky," Milton agreed, "but I guess it's all right just this once."

Val gave him a hug and a kiss. "I'm going to miss you, Milt the Stilt!" she said, laughing.

Before he could offer to shake her hand, too, Mrs. Racer bent down and kissed his cheek. "You're a good boy, Milton," she said. "Have a nice trip. Don't talk to strangers, and make sure the conductor tells you when you're coming into Penn Station so you have time to gather your things." She handed him a bulging paper bag. "Train food's terrible, I hear tell, so here's something to tide you over till you get home — some butterscotch brownies, two chicken sandwiches, some pickles, a hardboiled egg, an apple, and an orange. And plenty of paper napkins so you don't get crumbs all over your nice clothes."

"Thank you, Mrs. Racer," Milton said. "If I eat all that, I'll be as fat as Tiny. I'm glad you're going to adopt him. I'm sure you'll be very happy together."

"Hey, Milt, take care," said Teddy. "You know, when you first came, I thought you were hopeless, but you're okay. You're not really a wimp — or at least, not as much as you used to be."

"Teddy!" Doc and Val said together.

"That's okay. I *was* a wimp," Milton said cheerfully, "but I'm working on it. 'Bye, Ted. See you soon."

The two boys solemnly shook hands as the train pulled into the station. Doc picked up Milton's bags. "This is it. Come on, Milton, time to go."

Milton trotted after him. As he climbed into the car, he turned around and waved, and Val, Teddy, and Mrs. Racer waved back. A few minutes later, Doc returned to the platform and the train began to glide off down the track.

"Where is he? I don't see him," Teddy cried, staring up at the windows.

"There he is," Val said.

Milton's nose was pressed against the glass, and he was waving wildly.

"G'bye, Milt! See you soon!" Teddy shouted, jumping up and down and waving so hard Val thought his arm might fall right off. He waved until the train was out of sight. Then he sighed and his shoulders slumped a little.

"Miss him already, huh?" Val asked as they started up the steps to the waiting room.

"Well . . . kinda." He trudged beside her, head down. "I kinda got used to him, I guess."

"I don't suppose you could eat a little something," Mrs. Racer said.

Teddy brightened. "Like what?"

"Well, I brought along some extra butterscotch brownies, just in case." Mrs. Racer handed Teddy another brown paper bag.

"Oh, boy!" he crowed. "I was afraid you'd given 'em all to Milt! Hey, Dad, can we get some milk? We can eat these while we wait for Erin's train."

Doc smiled. "I think that could be arranged," he said.

Soon they were all seated on a bench in the waiting room, munching butterscotch brownies and drinking milk.

"Don't eat the last one, Teddy," Val said. "Save it for Erin. She hasn't had any of Mrs. Racer's goodies for ten whole days." She looked up at the clock at the end of the waiting room. Ten-thirty. Erin's train was due in at ten-fifty-six.

All of a sudden, Val couldn't wait to see her little sister. What with Milton and Tiny, she hadn't missed Erin as much as she'd thought she would, but now she was very impatient. Every time they'd spoken to Erin on the phone, she'd been bubbling over with excitement. And she'd been very good about sending postcards. Every day, one had arrived, usually with a picture of some famous ballet dancer on it, and filled with Erin's neat script: "Went to New York City Ballet at Lincoln Center with Aunt Peggy and Uncle John. *The Goldberg Variations* is absolutely *fantastic*! . . . Saw Suzanne Farrell dance *Slaughter on Tenth*

Avenue. She is the most beautiful dancer in the whole world! . . . Saw the Joffrey Ballet this afternoon. Really great! . . . Uncle John pulled some strings, and I actually took a class with the Joffrey. It was wonderful! . . . I *adore* Manhattan! From Aunt Peggy and Uncle John's windows you can see right across Central Park."

Mrs. Racer had put all the postcards up on the bulletin board on the back of the pantry door. It was a very colorful display. And now Erin was really coming home. Would she be different? Val wondered. Would she *look* different, *act* different? Milton had changed a lot over spring vacation. What if the Erin who stepped off the train wasn't the same Erin who'd left ten days ago?

Don't be silly! Val told herself. Erin's Erin. She remembered Mrs. Racer saying about Tiny, "Pigs are pigs." The thought made her smile. But she found that she couldn't finish the rest of her brownie. Her stomach was all tied in knots.

"Want this? I can't eat it all," she said to Teddy.

"You bet!" Teddy said, and gobbled it right up.

Doc checked his watch. "Let's toss our milk containers and these paper napkins in the garbage and start down to the platform. Erin's train will be coming in very soon."

"Y'know, I really want to see old Erin," Teddy

said. "She's been gone so long, I almost forget what she looks like."

Mrs. Racer frowned at him. "Your very own *sister*? Teddy Taylor, I'm ashamed of you! Erin'll look exactly the way she did when she left — like a little blonde angel. I bet she's lost weight," she worried. "Them New York folks don't know how to feed a body. Just look at Milton. Skinny as a rail when he arrived! But we'll fatten her up again. You still got that last brownie, Teddy?"

Teddy nodded.

"Good! And I've got a roast beef for a noon dinner and mashed potatoes and nice fresh vegetables, right off the farm. You don't get things like that in New York City." Mrs. Racer sniffed. "City folks don't know what good is!"

"I'm sure you're right, Mrs. Racer," Doc said, taking her arm. "Come on — we want to be right there when Erin gets off the train, so we can see her as soon as possible!" He winked at Val, and Val winked back.

"Wait till Erin meets Tiny!" Teddy said, charging down the steps. "She won't believe all the things he can do!"

Chapter 9

"Mrs. Racer, that was the very best meal I've had since I left for New York," Erin said a few hours later. They had just had dinner, and the Taylors were seated around the dining room table. Mrs. Racer had hovered over them every minute, making sure that nobody wanted for anything. Val, of course, had not eaten any of the roast beef, but she'd had her fill of vegetables and Mrs. Racer's extra-special dessert — chocolate fudge cake with big scoops of caramel nut ice cream from Curran's Dairy.

"I should hope so!" Mrs. Racer said. "Real home cooking, that's what you need. Put the roses back in your cheeks."

"Erin isn't exactly fading away," Doc said, smiling. "As a matter of fact, she looks positively blooming."

And she did. Val thought Erin looked older, somehow, and much more sophisticated. Maybe it was just because she hadn't seen her sister in ten days, but Erin's delicate features seemed finer, her eyes larger, her silvery blonde hair, pulled back as it usually was in a ballerina knot, glossier and more . . . perfect, was the only word Val could think of to describe it. She looked exactly like photographs of their mother — beautiful, kind of like a fairy-tale princess. In comparison, Val felt large and awkward. She was very conscious of the fact that her long chestnut hair kept straggling in front of her ears, no matter how often she tucked it back. But Erin hadn't really changed, she thought . . . had she?

"We had the most fabulous food," Erin said eagerly. "Aunt Peggy and Uncle John took me to these super restaurants, where the waiters treated you like royalty or something! And at the Adagio Cafe, in Lincoln Center, they have this wonderful buffet with every kind of food you can possibly imagine. The chefs wear big white aprons and tall white hats, and they serve you anything you want. Some of the stuff was really strange — like raw clams and oysters."

"Yuck!" Teddy said.

"I tried some, and it wasn't all that bad," Erin told him. "You know, the clams and oysters are still *alive* when you eat them, and they *quiver* when you squeeze lemon juice on them!"

"Yuck!" Val said, shivering. "You actually ate something that was *alive*?"

"I didn't like it much," Erin confessed. "As a matter of fact, I thought maybe I was going to throw up at first. But I didn't," she added proudly. "And in Japanese restaurants, they serve you raw fish! But it doesn't taste like fish. I think somebody ought to open a sushi bar in Essex. I bet it would be a sensation!"

Mrs. Racer shook her head. "It's not natural to eat raw fish."

"It wasn't nearly as good as your roast beef, Mrs. Racer," Erin said. "Oh, it's so nice to be home!"

"Is it?" Val asked quietly.

"Of course it is!" Erin said. "What's the matter with you, Vallie? You keep looking at me as if you've never seen me before."

Val shrugged, poking at the remains of her cake and ice cream. "It's just because you've never been away from home before, I guess. I never realized before how much you look like Mom."

"Well, what's so strange about that?" Erin asked. "I look like Mommy, and you look like Daddy, and Teddy — well, Teddy looks like both of them, I guess. Hey, Teddy, you're awfully quiet. Aren't you glad I'm home?"

"Yeah, I'm glad," Teddy said. "But you weren't very impressed with all the tricks Milt and me taught Tiny to do."

"Oh, Tiny!" Erin laughed. "Aunt Peggy and Uncle John couldn't *believe* you actually had a pig living in the house. I mean, in New York, people don't do things like that. But I told them that small town life is very different, and when your father's a vet, you get used to animals running around underfoot. Uncle John said he thought it was quaint."

"What's quaint mean?" Teddy asked suspiciously.

"Oh, kind of cute, funny — old-fashioned," Erin told him.

"Is that the way we seem to you — cute, funny, and old-fashioned?" asked Val.

Erin shrugged. "A little, I guess. Everything looks so different and kind of . . . *small* after New York. It'll take some getting used to."

Doc nodded. "Yes, I suppose it will."

Val stood up abruptly. "How about starting right now?" she said. "Come on, Erin — help me clear the table. Do you still remember how to stack the dishes in the dishwasher?"

"Now, Vallie, you let Erin take it easy," Mrs. Racer said. "The poor child's just had a long train trip. Teddy and me will clean up, won't we, Teddy?"

"That's okay, Mrs. Racer," Erin said. "I'm not tired, not a bit. And then I'll give everybody the presents I bought. It's such fun shopping in New York! You wouldn't *believe* the stores, Vallie. When I go back this summer, you have to come with me. Aunt Peggy says that Teddy's coming to visit Milton, and she wants us to come, too. It's going to be super!"

"Gee, Erin, you just got here, and now you're talking about going away again," Teddy grumbled, following his sisters into the kitchen with his dessert plate and fork.

"It sounds to me like you're homesick for New York," Val added sadly.

"Don't be silly, Vallie." Erin began putting the plates into the dishwasher. "You can't be homesick for a place that's not your home. But it will be someday, when I'm a famous ballerina!"

"Mom was pretty famous, but *she* didn't live in New York," Val reminded her. "She stayed right here in Pennsylvania and married Dad."

"And a good thing she did, too," said Mrs. Racer, "or else where would you three be, I'd like to know?"

"Hey, what about those presents?" Teddy put in. "Are you going to give them to us now?"

"Yes, I sure am." Erin ran into the dining room. "Daddy, where's that big Bloomingdale's shopping bag? Everything's in there. Come on, everybody — come into the living room and sit down."

Doc gave her the shopping bag, and Erin began happily handing around her gifts. There was a brass paperweight in the shape of a dog for Doc, a baseball yearbook for Teddy, a lavender silk scarf for Mrs. Racer, and a silver horseshoe pin for Val.

"I bought myself a present, too," Erin confessed, unrolling a New York City Ballet poster. "I'm going to hang it right over my bed — or maybe on the wall across from my bed, so I can look at it before I go to sleep and when I wake up."

After everyone had thanked her for their gifts, Doc carried Erin's suitcase up to her room. Teddy went out to play with his friends, and Mrs. Racer went back to the kitchen, where Tiny was curled up under the butcher block table, sound asleep.

Val, feeling at loose ends, wandered upstairs and plopped down on her sister's bed. Dandelion was singing his head off, much to Erin's delight.

"He didn't sing much while you were gone," Val said. "I guess he missed you a lot. I don't think Milton paid much attention to Dandy."

"I'm glad," Erin said. "I was afraid maybe he'd forget all about me."

She began changing out of her dress and into her leotard and tights.

"As soon as I unpack, I'm going to call Olivia and see if she can come over. I have a present for her, too, and I have so much to tell her! And then I'll show her some of the things we did in that ballet class I took. We can practice together."

"Oh," said Val. "I thought maybe you'd like to come out with me to Animal Inn. We could ride The Ghost for a while. Olivia could come, too."

"Thanks, Vallie, but not today. Except for that one class, I've hardly done my exercises at all, and my legs feel stiff as a board. Until Olivia gets here, I want to go down to the basement and warm up. But say hi to The Ghost for me."

"Yeah, I will." Val started out of Erin's room, then paused and turned back. "Erin. . . ."

"What?"

"Are you *really* glad to be home?"

"Sure I am," Erin said, wriggling into her leotard. "Don't you believe me?"

"Yes, I believe you," Val said. But as she left the room, she wasn't completely sure she did.

"Hiya, Vallie. Come out to see The Ghost?" Mike Strickler asked when Val came into the barn about half an hour later. She'd left her bike outside, and was on her way to The Ghost's tack room to get his saddle and bridle.

"That's right, Mike," she said.

"Erin get home all right?"

"Yes. She had a wonderful time in New York City."

Val lugged the saddle and bridle into The Ghost's stall and began tacking him up.

"What's the matter, Vallie?" Mike asked, leaning on his pitchfork. "You look kinda down in the mouth."

Val tightened the girth and buckled it. "Oh, I don't know. . . . Yes, I do. It's Erin. I was afraid she'd change, and she has. I don't think anybody else has noticed it, but *I* do."

"Changed? How do you mean? Like citified?"

Val nodded. "You got it, Mike. She's citified, all right. She thinks we're *quaint*!" She slipped the bridle over The Ghost's head.

"Quaint, huh?" Mike mulled that over. "Maybe we are, at that. Don't seem such a bad thing to be."

"Yes, but it was the way she said it that got me," Val said, leading The Ghost out of his stall. "Like *we* were separate from *her*. And we're not! We're all the same family."

" 'Course you are." Mike patted her on the shoulder. "She'll come around, Vallie, just you wait and see. You have a nice ride now, clear the cobwebs out of your head. I bet when you get back home, Erin'll be just like she was before she left."

Val swung up into the saddle. "I sure hope you're right, Mike." She smiled down at the little old man. "See you later." She nudged The Ghost's glossy gray sides with her heels and headed out of the barn. Riding her horse always made her feel good, no matter what was bothering her. Talking to Mike had made her feel better, too. And it was a beautiful spring afternoon. Imagine Erin preferring to practice ballet exercises down in the basement on a day like this! She clucked to The Ghost, urging him into a brisk trot.

"I'm probably getting all worked up over nothing," she told the horse as they ambled down a country lane. She took a deep breath of the sweet spring air. "No more cobwebs," she added, and The Ghost flicked his ears back and forth as though he agreed.

That evening, Val bade a fond farewell to Tiny. Mrs. Racer's son Henry was taking the piglet to Mrs. Racer's farm — though Mrs. Racer said he wasn't too happy about having a pig in his car.

"But I told him it wasn't sensible to bring the truck for one little pig," she said. " 'Pretend he's a dog,' I told him. His dogs ride in the car all the time."

A horn honked outside.

"There he is. Time to go, little feller." Mrs. Racer tugged gently on the rope that Teddy had tied around Tiny's neck, and the piglet trotted along beside her.

"I'm gonna miss that pig," Teddy said wistfully, watching Tiny clamber into the back seat of Henry's car. "Me and Milt had a lot of fun with him."

"I'll miss him, too," said Val. "Pigs are really good pets."

"But Tiny will be much happier with other pigs around," Doc said. "And you know that Mrs. Racer will be glad to have you come visit him whenever you like."

"Frankly, I'm just as glad he's gone," Erin said. "Oh, Vallie, don't look at me that way. He's a perfectly nice pig, but I hardly got to know him, and even *you* must admit it's kind of peculiar to have a pig running around the house. Olivia didn't say anything when she saw him in the living room, but I could tell she thought it was weird."

Doc sat down in his favorite chair and picked up the newspaper. "Well, honey, I think I can promise you that Tiny, besides being the *first* pig we ever had as a houseguest, will also be the last. You'll be able to hold your head up in front of your friends from now on."

"Well, it *was* a little embarrassing," Erin said. "They don't allow any pets at all in Aunt Peggy and Uncle John's building."

"Not even canaries?" Teddy asked.

"I'm not sure about that," Erin replied. "But I'm absolutely positive about pigs! When I grow up and move to New York — "

"Oh, Erin, can't you talk about anything else?" Val burst out. "Ever since you got home, all you can think about is how great it is in New York! You sound like you're sorry you had to come back. Mike's right — you sure are citified!"

"Calm down, Vallie," Doc said, putting down his paper. "Give Erin a chance to readjust. It's not surprising that Essex seems like the wild frontier compared to the life Erin's been living for the past ten days."

"But it's *not* the wild frontier," Val protested. "It's home! It's Erin's home as well as yours and Teddy's and mine."

Erin sighed. "Vallie, don't you think I know that? But just because it's home doesn't mean it's absolutely perfect."

"I think it is," Val said quietly. "I never want to live anywhere else."

"Me, neither," Teddy added. "Y'know," he said, looking thoughtfully at Erin, "I've been thinking. When Milton came, he was such an uptight city kid he just about made me puke. . . ." He caught Doc's eye and quickly said, "I mean, throw up. But when he left, he'd turned into an okay guy. And when you went away, Erin, you were okay, and now that you're back, you're an uptight city kid. Maybe you and Milton oughta change places. Maybe Milton oughta move in with us, and you oughta go live with Aunt Peggy and Uncle John."

Erin's eyes widened and instantly brimmed with tears.

"Teddy!" she gasped. "Do you want to trade me for *Milton*?"

"Well, I don't *want* to, 'zactly," Teddy mumbled, "but it looks like that's what *you* want."

Erin flew across the room and flung herself into Doc's arms. "Daddy, Teddy wants to trade me in like — like a used car or something!" she wailed.

"And Vallie's mad at me! Doesn't anybody love me anymore?"

Jocko and Sunshine, who had been sitting quietly by until now, leaped to their feet and began barking madly. Cleveland, startled out of his snooze on the sofa, arched his back and bristled his tail like a Halloween cat. Val grabbed him and smoothed his ruffled fur.

"I'm not mad at you, Erin," she said around the lump that had suddenly formed in her throat. "You're my sister and I love you very much." She buried her nose in Cleveland's thick coat. "But I was afraid you'd be different when you came back, and you are. And I just want everything to be the way it was before you left!"

"Vallie, come here." Doc stood up, holding Erin with one arm and stretching out the other to Val. "You, too, Teddy."

Val put Cleveland down, and she and Teddy came over to Doc and Erin. Somehow, they all managed to huddle in Doc's embrace.

"Erin," he said gently, "this isn't the kind of homecoming any of us had anticipated. You're suffering from what's called culture shock, I think, and the rest of us are in the same boat. We want you to be the same little girl you've always been — I guess we don't really want you to grow up. And that's wrong. Everybody has to grow, and I don't mean just getting bigger and smarter. The problem is that you've grown up a lot in a very short time, and it's going to take the rest of us a while to realize it."

Erin wiped her streaming eyes on Doc's shirt front.

"But Teddy said. . . ." She gulped.

"That was just a tease," Teddy said. "I don't really want to trade you in for Milton. Like I said, Milt's shaping up pretty good, but I wouldn't want him to live here all the time." He looked up at Erin and grinned. "We had real lousy breakfasts while you were gone, Erin. Milt can't cook at all, and Vallie always burns the bacon!"

"Val burns everything — even microwaved bacon!" Erin said.

"Yeah, I do," Val said, hugging her sister. "I'm a rotten cook. But that's not the only reason I'm glad you're back. If you really want me to, I'll go to New York with you this summer to visit Aunt Peggy and Uncle John. I want to find out what's so great about living in a big city, so when you're a famous ballerina, I'll enjoy coming to visit you in your apartment, even if you can't have any pets."

Erin sniffed. "I'll *never* live anywhere where I can't have a canary. And if you bring a pig along, well, I'll work it out somehow."

Val couldn't help laughing through her tears. "I

promise I'll *never* bring a pig along! But I just might bring Cleveland."

Doc hugged all his children as tightly as he could.

"Welcome home, Erin," he said gruffly.

"Welcome home," Val echoed.

"Yeah, welcome home. Isn't it about suppertime?" Teddy asked, pulling away. "I'm starvin'. . . ."

"Like Marvin. Me, too!" Erin laughed, a little shakily. "I'll fix us all something to eat. Want to help me, Vallie?"

"Sure — why not?" Val put her arm around her sister and squeezed her tight. "And after supper, you can help me feed the rabbits."

The sisters headed for the kitchen, arm in arm.